RUG MAN

RUG MAN

DAVID AMADIO

PAUL DRY BOOKS
Philadelphia 2023

First Paul Dry Books Edition, 2023

Paul Dry Books, Inc.
Philadelphia, Pennsylvania
www.pauldrybooks.com

"Tools of the Trade": Illustration by Debra Burke

ISBN: 978-1-58988-173-0

Printed in the United States of America

Library of Congress Control Number: 2022951098

for my father

The soul of the apartment is the carpet. From it are deduced not only the hues but the forms of all objects incumbent. A judge at common law may be an ordinary man; a good judge of a carpet must be a genius.

—EDGAR ALLAN POE

. . . the night cometh, when no man can work.

—JOHN 9:4

RUG MAN

CHAPTER ONE

Frank Renzetti pulled up to the house on Dunwoody Lane, grabbed a tape measure from the dashboard of his van, and stepped out into the bog of late July, the air dead to everything but the whirring cicada. He climbed the long driveway: to his right, a line of commercial vehicles— each one belonging to a different contractor—stretched from the garage to the sidewalk; to his left, in the middle of the front yard, stood an old silver maple with a massive burl at the base of its trunk. A brown-necked landscaper, the cuffs of his jeans pasted with grass clippings, patted the knot and spoke to it softly. Frank couldn't make out what the man was saying, but his tone was earnest, sad even, and the sight of him made Frank want to turn around and get back in the van. If they were talking to trees on the lawn, who knew what they were doing behind closed doors.

Elaine George, the decorator, had asked Frank to come out this morning for one last walk-through. He had measured the job back in January, and the rugs had been sitting in his warehouse for almost a month, still in their packaging. Elaine, like many of the decorators he had worked for over the years, couldn't schedule to save her life, and the chaos she courted often got in the way of her expertise. Ideally, the carpet installer is last on the job, after the carpenters and the painters and the electricians have all cleared out. The vans in the driveway and the trucks on the street told Frank that he was not going to be alone. He had hoped for something different, but he was never one to live too long in hope. It only postponed the suffering.

He paused at the top of the driveway and looked at the house. It was a Neo-Colonial, built in 2005 as part of the Heatherstone development, a gated community in Villanova, the heart of Philly's posh Main Line. The homeowner, Connie Silberstein, had divorced her attorney husband Norm Kershner almost a year ago and hired Elaine George and a general contractor named Vic Satrapini to help her remodel the place. Much of the renovation was going on inside, but Frank saw that the stone masons had given the front of the house a fieldstone facelift. The carpenters had also been busy out here, replacing the portico's rounded columns with square, fluted ones. The windows were now double-hung with louvered shutters, and the architectural shingles were now slate. It must be nice, thought Frank, to only have to worry about how the money goes out. The Heatherstone houses had all been cut from the same mold, with only a few differences to set them apart. It seemed Connie was doing everything she could to give the house an identity, so that onlookers would never think to call it a McMansion, or worse, the house where Norm Kershner once lived.

Frank stood in the colonnaded entranceway and knocked on the door. No one answered, so he knocked again, and again no one came. He could hear a radio playing in the foyer, and men yelling deep within the house. The radio was tuned to 1080 the Squawker, a conservative station, and the voice on the air was yelling, too, as if the house and the radio were an echo of each other. After his third knock went unanswered, Frank let himself in. The security system beeped two times loudly and proclaimed in a generic female voice, "Front door open."

At the far end of the foyer, standing on an A-frame ladder, a painter was cutting in the topmost corner of a double-vaulted tray ceiling. He was balancing on one foot, his body angled away from the wall, his free hand gripping the side of the ladder. Another painter walked into the foyer with a five-gallon bucket of primer and set it on a drop cloth with the rest of their supplies: rollers, paint sticks, a medley of brushes soaking in a can of mineral spirits.

"How ya' doin'?" said Frank to the second painter, who was popping open the primer with a flat-head screwdriver.

"Another day in paradise," he said, eyes on his work.

"Is Elaine around?" Frank asked.

"Last time I saw her she was in the kitchen." He said this with a needle, a quick derision.

"Thanks," said Frank, and turned right into the dining room.

Over by the window, a carpenter was getting ready to cut a strip of molding with a table saw. A thin sheet of plastic covered the dining room table, but there were holes in it where saw dust had collected in little blonde drifts. The carpenter wore a faded cap over his shaggy gray hair and a suede tool pouch on his hip. Measuring what he needed, he slid a flat pencil from behind his ear and struck a line on the molding. Then he raised the safety guard on the saw and pulled the trigger. The blade bit into the wood, and for ten seconds all Frank knew was the buzz and blur of it tearing across the grain. It spun to a stop and the carpenter gave Frank a weary nod, the gesture a tally of the months he'd spent entombed in the house. Carpenters are longest on any job, their reserves as shallow as their wounds are deep. Frank nodded back and continued through the butler's pantry into the kitchen.

Men were drilling handles into glass-front cabinet doors, and beyond them, on the other side of the island, a tile-layer set travertine squares in the morning room. From the planning center, a cubby off the kitchen, out swung Elaine George. The designer, in her late forties, had blonde, curly hair and a full face, with something of the fat cartoon mouse in her cheeks and chin. Red-framed glasses clung to the tip of her nose, and it seemed as if the slightest bump would knock them from their perch. She was talking to someone on her phone about towel bars, and it sounded like the person on the other end was not telling her what she wanted to hear. She waved to Frank, signaling that she'd only be a minute. Pacing the length of the kitchen in her black high heels, she tried to lift her voice above the squeal of the drill and the scrape of the trowel, but her words were eaten by the noise. She hung up with a grimace.

"Hey, Frank," she said, acknowledging him over the tops of her glasses.

Frank and Elaine had been working together for over six years. Theirs was a business relationship, fixed and formal. They got along well, and this was due to a total lack of interest in each other's personal lives. He knew that she lived in progressive, bespoke Narberth and had a teenage daughter who had just graduated from The Agnes Irwin School, and she knew that he had been married for thirty-seven years and lived in a modest split-level in Broomall. Beyond that, they were strangers and more than content to keep it that way.

"Follow me," she said.

Elaine led him into the rear foyer and opened the double doors to the study. The room had once been Norm Kershner's office, but after he moved out Connie claimed it for herself and made it the focal point of the renovation. Both she and Elaine referred to it as the "sanctuary."

"The rug for here is coming next Thursday," said Elaine, "by cargo ship. I want you to pick it up at the Pennsport docks. I don't want it passing through anyone else's hands but yours."

Such a logistical circumvention was unusual for Frank, but then so was the rug. For months, Elaine and Connie had deliberated over the style, the make, the color, the size. Connie wanted something new that felt and looked old; Elaine wanted something old that felt and looked new. They settled on a reproduction of an antique Sarouk prayer rug from the fifteenth century. It was called Timeless Peacock, and they spoke about it as if it had magical powers, as if Connie could sit upon its center medallion, chant a few words in Farsi, and be swept away on a zephyr to the hills of Azerbaijan.

"The furniture is arriving on Friday afternoon," Elaine said. "I want you to lay the rug before it gets here, preferably that morning, early."

Frank looked at the side windows and frowned at the sunlight beating in unfiltered.

"Are you doing window treatments?" he asked.

"Eventually," said Elaine. "Why?"

"You might have some oxidation issues if you don't."

"Really?" A note of panic entered her voice. "To the artificial dye?"

"It won't happen overnight," he explained, "but it'll happen."

In Frank's mouth, the word "oxidation" meant a gradual lightening of color due to prolonged exposure to the sun's rays, but in Connie's ears, which rotated like a cat's whenever bad news was about, it meant the Rapture.

"We're doing yurdmas in the family room," she said, half to herself. "They're on the denser side. They cut down on light. We could do them in here, too. I'll have to ask Connie."

Frank didn't know what a yurdma was, but he nodded anyway, guessing it was drapery of some kind, twee curtains Elaine had discovered in the back room of some little shop, forgotten for reasons soon to be known by the one she'd hire to hang them.

"Let's go upstairs," she said.

As they were leaving the room, Frank ran his hand over the fabric-lined wallpaper. It felt like the skin of a peach, had convexity, and when he pressed on it firmly, a sponginess. It was as if someone had taken a padded room and painted it blue. Frank was confused. Are you seeking refuge, he wondered, or are you being committed? *In this house*, the sanctuary seemed to answer, *there is no difference*.

Connie had two daughters, Miranda and Rachel. Elaine urged Frank to measure their rooms again, to account for any discrepancies. He did this reluctantly, jotting down the numbers in his pocket notebook as an empty show of courtesy. After re-measuring the guest bedroom and the loft, he followed Elaine into the master, where two electricians were fumbling with a ceiling fan.

"Any problems?" she asked.

"Not yet," said the man on the ladder, whose forearms were sleeved in tattoos. His apprentice stood off to the side, a gofer on call, waiting to be told which item to produce from the great leather bag on the floor.

Frank worked around them, measuring the length and width of the space, and then went back to the walk-in closet, where he found Connie's housekeeper dusting the valet table. She was a thin, pale woman with concave cheeks and short, flat hair like a boy. When she saw Frank, she quickened her dusting.

"Excuse me," she said in a respectful brogue. "I'll get out of your way."

"Take your time," said Frank.

He knew better than to rush a housekeeper. They did a fine job of hiding it, but they were the true seats of power in any home. Their dominion stretched from the attic to the basement, and of every corner and crevice they had intimate knowledge. They knew where everything was and how everything worked, and could grant you access to things if you stayed on their good side.

"I'm Frank," he said.

"Gildea. Nice to meet you." With her raw-knuckled hands she snatched her caddy of cleansers and rags and, in a soft swish of scrubs, lightly made her exit.

A bit on the frail side, Frank observed, but certainly not one to be crossed.

He double-checked the closet's dimensions, and, for a

moment, stood looking at Connie's floor-to-ceiling wall of shoes. Not just a collector of footwear, Connie was a curator, separating boots from heels, flats from wedges, Jimmy from Cole, and further grouping them according to color. Frank guessed there were over sixty pairs in all, far more than his wife owned, far, *far* more. Faced with such a glut, he regretted ever having given Donna grief. The next time he felt the need to complain about the size of her wardrobe, he would think of Connie Silberstein, and keep his mouth shut.

On their way downstairs, Frank and Elaine stopped on the landing, which was long enough and wide enough to be its own room.

"Bound sisal for the steps, landing, and upper hall," she said. "And we're showing the same amount of wood all around: five inches. Did I tell you about the new mill?"

"No," Frank said flatly.

"This time I ordered the sisal from Kenya, and the guy who runs the mill, Alex Odondo, told me about the life of the agave plant in eastern Africa. After three years of having its leaves cut and harvested, it sprouts a green stalk as tall and as thick as a telephone pole—one last effort at growth before they torch the stems and re-seed the ground for the next harvest. Isn't that amazing?"

Again, Frank could only nod. He would never say it aloud, but there was something he wished to tell Connie about her revolutionary strand: it's hell to apply. After a long day of working with sisal, his knees looked and felt as if they'd been branded with a waffle iron. And for what? It had all the charm and comfort of a straw mat, one that was hard to clean, frayed incessantly, and prickled the soles of bare-footed children. Frank tried, but for the life of him he could not see the attraction to sisal. Until it was no longer his lot to wrestle such goods, their appeal would remain a mystery to him.

"Connie didn't want sisal at first," said Elaine, "but I talked her into it. It's just the right touch of 'wabi' on these steps. Have you looked at it yet?"

"I took a peek," Frank said. "I'll get a better look this afternoon when I start to pre-fab."

Elaine's body tensed, and her voice sounded that same note of panic as before. "You're just cutting, right? You're not doing any sewing or binding at your shop?"

"I was planning on doing *all* the sewing and binding at the shop. There's too much going on here for me to do it on-site."

"I understand, but Connie wants everything done in the house. The cabinet makers put the handles on ahead of time and she got really upset. She said they placed them too high. I had to ask the guys to re-set them, and even then she wasn't happy."

Frank didn't expect Elaine to admit how preposterous this was, but it didn't stop him from thinking that maybe she should.

"Didn't you say that she was staying with her sister this week?"

"She was going to," said Elaine, "but then they got this new dog, and the brother-in-law is allergic, so Connie and the girls are just going to tough it out here."

"Elaine!" called a man's throaty voice. "Did you order the finial?"

"Not yet," she said, quickly descending the last flight of stairs, Frank trailing behind. "What did she finally decide?"

"The topaz ball from Grand Forge," said the man, who was standing in the foyer with his arms folded across his chest. "You better overnight it. She wants it by Monday."

"Frank," said Elaine, "this is Vic Satrapini. Have the two of you met?"

"Not formally," said Frank, reaching out his hand. "I don't think you were here the first time I measured."

"Oh, I was here," Vic assured him, enveloping Frank's hand in his and giving it a strong squeeze.

The general contractor was a big man, tall, red, and fleshy. One had to look up to meet his pessimistic eyes, which were shadowed by the ridge of his knotted, black brow. He stunk of burnt garlic and stale cologne, and sucked air through his blubbery mouth when he wasn't speaking. A real *padrone*.

"Frank's doing the carpets," said Elaine. "He'll be here about a week."

"Any muchachos working for you?" Vic asked.

Frank thought that this was an odd question, and he lingered a moment before answering. "No," he said. "My guys are . . . American."

"Good," said Vic, the hawsers folding again. "I don't want any muchachos in the house. Last big job I did, two Mexican carpet guys stole a bunch of shit from the garage. Golf clubs, ski poles. The people were *livid*. That's Manuel labor for you."

"Is Connie back yet?" Elaine asked Vic.

"No, she's still dropping the girls off at camp."

Just then, a fawn-coated pug hustled out of the powder room with a wax toilet ring clenched in its mouth. A plumber, looking not at all exasperated, shuffled after the dog and calmly removed the ring. The pug flattened its rose-shaped ears and looked up expectantly at the plumber. It was wheezing from the short-lived chase.

"Second time it's happened this morning," said the plumber. "P.J. thinks it's a toy."

"He thinks everything's a toy," Vic said bitterly.

"Did Connie walk him before she left?" Elaine asked.

"I have no idea," said Vic.

P.J. sat back with his hind legs spread, then, using his front legs to propel himself forward, scooted across the floor, leaving behind a foot-long skid mark on the painter's drop-cloth, brown and pasty and fairly straight.

"Get the fuck outta here!" Vic boomed, and P.J. ran into the dining room, his curlicue tail waving a stiff goodbye. "Dog doesn't give a shit about anything. The tile guy said he caught him rolling around in the wet grout yesterday. If you look, you can see hairs in it. And he scratched the shower enclosure."

"Sacs on either side of his behind are enflamed," said the plumber. "My Jack Russell had it. Only gets worse if you don't have him checked out."

Elaine looked at the skid mark and then at Frank, one corner of her mouth attempting a smile, her small shoulders slumped. "We'll take care of it," she said. "No way he's doing that on the new carpet."

Frank joined her outside beneath the portico, and they went over some final details before Elaine surrendered to the heat and promised Frank that she'd see him first thing Monday morning.

"And don't mind Vic," she said. "He's kind of a bully." She bent forward, her glasses holding on by a miracle of friction, and whispered loud enough for Frank to hear. "I was on that job where the golf clubs were stolen, and I can assure you that the carpet guys didn't do it. The oldest son sold them and didn't tell his parents."

"Does Vic know that?" Frank asked.

"Yes, but he doesn't believe it." She lay a hand on one of the newly minted columns and intensified her whisper. "Vic needs something to give people a hard time about. Just let him have his crusade, or he'll start looking for somebody else to go after."

Back in the van, Frank wedged the tape measure between the dashboard and windshield and checked his flip phone: no calls, no messages—just the time. He took his keys from beneath the seat and started the engine. Then he sat back and ran the numbers: five bedrooms; four walk-in closets; 200 feet of carpet; 100 of cotton binding; and six rolls of ¾-inch felt pad. It was more material and more work than Frank had seen in months, and he was grateful for it ("You're going to need something substantial this summer," his accountant had told him, "just to stay afloat"), but he questioned whether his skeleton crew was enough to carry the day. He thought of his mechanic, Billy, and his gofer, Kyle, and considered hiring another hand, another body to move furniture, bag up scraps, and haul the old carpet to the curb. Picking up someone on short notice wouldn't be easy, and picking up someone reliable—someone *good*—would be asking for the moon. Of all the trades, the carpet industry was cursed with the shallowest pool of day laborers, and the thought of dipping into it made Frank sick.

The general contractor walked out of the house and barked a few words at the landscaper. The man slumped off and Vic went over to the port-a-potty at the top of the driveway. Frank watched him throw open the door and read a small chart on the inside that logged the unit's pick-up and service dates. Vic slammed the door shut and kicked the port-a-potty as hard as he could with the sole of his work boot, nearly knocking it over. Then he called someone on his phone, switching it from ear to ear as he stalked back and forth like a predator.

In his many years of laying carpet, Frank had run his share of marathons (the Palmieri job in Rittenhouse Square, the Rifkin job in Bala), tournaments of will and strength for which great stores of patience had been emptied. But this job—before he had even made a single cut—this job felt different: bigger, louder, stranger. This could be it, he thought—the one to send me packing.

He felt the damp suck of cotton against the small of his back and realized he was sweating. It was hot inside the van—*blood* hot. He turned on the air conditioner, listened to it recall the purpose of its one earthly task, and drove out of Heatherstone.

CHAPTER TWO

Windsor Carpets had been in Frank Renzetti's family since 1962, the year his Uncle John began cleaning and repairing Oriental rugs out of a small garage in Jenkintown. John, his father's youngest brother, had always been Frank's favorite uncle, so it was no surprise when the eager nephew, looking for something better than swing shift at the Navy Yard to support his wife and three-month-old son, went to work for John as an apprentice in the summer of 1983. By this time, John had moved Windsor's base of operations from Jenkintown to Folcroft, a working-class suburb southwest of Philadelphia, and expanded the business to installation and sales. During the Reagan era, customers wanted wall-to-wall, deep-pile carpeting in every room of the house, their footfalls cushioned by the plush nap of Dupont Stainmaster in colors like Morning Rose Petal and Seafoam Green. It was in this crucible that Frank learned the trade, guided by his uncle's patient yet exacting hand. John Renzetti, fearing it might die with him if he did not hand it down, bequeathed to Frank the Windsor way of putting in the goods: how to mold a rug to

fit the contours of a bull-nosed step; how to hammer tackless stripping without gouging the baseboard; how to trim
the raw selvage from two identical carpets, so that when it
came time to fuse them with a hot seaming iron, the junc-
ture would be invisible.

There was craft in the work, true skill, but it was hard
on the body, draining of all one had to give and then
demanding still more. Each day, Frank went home in a
doleful haze, nicked and bruised and blistered, nursing an
ache that was almost pleasant, tired to the point of laughing. He would look down and his hands and knees would
be red and swollen. He would wake in the morning and
there would be few parts of him that did not hurt. He
came from the same stock as his Uncle John, but he began
to doubt his share of that rugged man's blood. Over time,
his body accepted the job and its strain, allowing itself to
be hewn and wrought by it. His shoulders, back, and legs
grew stronger, and the muscles of his arms annealed in
the dry room of the company plant, where he would drape
the ends of unwieldy rugs still wet from shampooing over
spiked wooden poles and hoist them to the ceiling, pulling hand over hand on a thick yellow rope until the whit-
ened fringes were clear of the ground and the fans could
be turned upon them.

It didn't take long for Frank to graduate from apprentice
to mechanic. John had another man on the payroll, a gan-
gly motormouth named Chick who often showed up late
and whose answer to the job's more stressful requirements
was always, "I picked a helluva profession to get into, didn't
I?" For all his complaining, Chick did very little actual
work, which meant that Frank had to take up the slack,
blindly, bravely, daring his hands to perform new tasks.

This did not go unnoticed by John. He saw in his nephew a zeal and a talent, and because this combination of traits was so rare in his business, he rewarded Frank with a raise and a nickname. The raise comforted Frank, but the nickname—"Ace"—lifted him up, made him feel exceptional. For he loved his uncle: he loved his lenient perfectionism ("It looks good from Folcroft"), his low profile, and his stoic disregard of other men's wealth. There was a musty cool in this rug man's obscurity, and the name "Ace" granted some of that cool to Frank, labeling him a disciple of a particular style of manual labor and positioning him as John's contemporary. Only when the occasion called for it would nephew and uncle use their proper names; in all other exchanges they referred to each other as "Ace," their casual acknowledgment of mutual mastery.

Fifteen years they worked together, until John's ailing wife called him home for the last time, and it was a favor to him that she did because John's knees had had enough. With help from Donna's parents, Frank bought the business from John in 1998. The following year a commercial property came on the market, a warehouse in Upper Darby that had once belonged to a sprinkler company and before that a manufacturer of single-engine plane propellers. Even John would admit that the space in Folcroft was something of a barn, drafty and damp and verminous. In the late nineties, Windsor was regularly doing work for Main Line decorators. Axeminster carpet was being shipped from overseas and Frank needed a bigger, cleaner plant in which to cut and sew and bind. The warehouse in Upper Darby satisfied that need. Drawing up to it now in his van, the building looked much the same as it did when Frank had first moved in: long, low, deep, and wide, a crème brulee rectangle squatting beneath a flat roof, its left side scaled with tumbles of English ivy, the garage door trim showing mahogany in the sunlight. It had caused him agita over the years (wide cracks in the cement walls, ground water pooling after a heavy rain), but not so much that it became a burden. He had spent so much of his life in this warehouse—more than he had spent in the home he shared with his wife—and while this might gnaw at the conscience of another man, forcing him to reconsider the value of his sacrifice, Frank merely thought that work must be done somewhere, and here is the place that I've chosen to do mine.

He backed up to the mouth of the open garage and stopped just shy of the threshold. He had parked the van like this so many times before that he no longer needed to look at his mirrors; instinct alone docked the vessel in its slip. He left the keys beneath the seat and walked into the air-conditioned office. Billy Norway was sitting in a chair by the door, eating cream-chipped beef from a Styrofoam container. Billy's nephew Kyle stood next to him with a Red Bull and a cigarette, playing a video on his smartphone of two girls fighting in a school parking lot.

"The best part," snorted Kyle, "is when her one titty comes out the bottom of her shirt and her other titty comes out the top."

Frank sat at his desk and switched on the brass reading lamp. He slid Connie's floor plan from a stack of papers, many bearing room schematics he had drafted by hand. He compared the numbers in his notebook to the ones he had written on the plan months earlier: they were identical. He plucked a pen from an old mason jar and started listing measurements on a small yellow legal pad, trying to block out the raunch of Billy and Kyle's laughter. He was relieved when the video abruptly ended and Kyle sat in a folding chair on the other side of the room.

"What time did you get here?" Frank asked them.

"Half hour ago," said Billy. He wiped his mouth with the hem of his shirt and lit a cigarette. Now the room had two strata of smoke. "How'd it go at Silberstein's?" he asked.

Frank continued writing on the legal pad. "It went all right," he said. "GC's kind of a hard-ass, and of course Elaine's got everybody in there at once. Typical clown house."

Kyle chuckled at something on his phone. Frank stopped writing and turned his head, thinking the kid was laughing at him. Kyle looked up from the screen, puffed apart the wings of greasy brown hair curtaining his eyes, and took a long, squinty drag on his cigarette. Feeling the judgment in Frank's gaze, he discretely blew the smoke out the side of his mouth and sat up straighter in his seat.

Kyle was a high school dropout, and—in Frank's opinion—had no future except the one that was right in front of his face. Billy's sister lived in the Poconos and had sent Kyle to stay with his uncle after he had gotten arrested a few times for petty offenses. She knew he was doing drugs and suspected that he was selling them, too. Billy hadn't been her first choice, but he was the only relative within driving distance willing to take Kyle in. To keep him out of trouble, Billy had started bringing Kyle into work a few days a week. He showed no interest in learning how to install carpet, and spent much of the day waiting for Frank to tell him what to do, loitering in hallways or gazing out windows, continually snapping the rubber bands he wore on both his wrists.

"How about the homeowner?" Billy asked. "You meet her?"

"No," Frank replied, "but from what Elaine was telling me, she's a real piece of work. She wants us to do all the binding and sewing at the house."

He tore the sheet from the legal pad and handed it to Billy. "The first three cuts are off the 60-foot roll at the top of the pile," he said. "You got one at 12 by 25 and one at 12 by 14. The second one's for the walk-in closet. The closet's only 11 feet wide. No seams in there."

Billy studied the paper through a scrim of white smoke, nodding each time that Frank ticked off a number.

"The next three are for the stairs and the second-floor hall. It's sisal, so you'll need the wheel to get through it. Whatever you have left after the third cut, that's what we'll use for the landing."

As Billy and Kyle made their way out to the warehouse floor, Frank nudged his high-backed rolling chair closer to the desk, pushed play on the office phone's answering machine, and listened to the first of two messages.

"Hello, Mr. Renzetti. This is Amanda, and I'm calling to remind you that there's still time to reserve your spot in the Google Marketplace. The world of business is changing, and you don't want to be left behind. Many of your competitors have already signed up! If you don't act soon to create a digital outpost for your company, they will lure away any potential new customers—the one thing *all* businesses need to survive. To keep your brand fresh, and to make your services are available to the twenty-first-century consumer, please call me back at extension 4422 so we can discuss the details of your Marketplace account. Thank you, and I hope you have a wonderful day."

This Amanda had called once last week and twice the week before. She was the latest telemarketer in a decade-long campaign to sell Frank on the bounty of e-commerce. First they told him he needed to computerize his records, then they told him he needed a website, now they were telling him he needed to join the virtual bazaar. Thanks to caller ID, he knew when the salvos were coming in. After a few weeks of unreturned calls, they would usually relent and move on to the next guy. Amanda, though, she was persistent. Frank had begun listening to her messages all the way through, something he had rarely done for her predecessors. The slight rasp in her voice, the sexy sincerity of her spiel, kept Frank's finger frozen above the erase button. It sounded as if she were telling him about the future of his love life, not the future of his company. He would miss her when she finally gave up on him.

The second message was from Janet Malloy, one of Frank's oldest and dearest customers. He had inherited Janet from his uncle; she went as far back as the Jenkintown days. A widow, she lived alone in a manor house in Chestnut Hill that she had been trying to sell for the past three years. Janet was in her late seventies and was an original member of Windsor's Summer Rug Gang.

"Good morning, Frank," the message began. "I hope you're having a fine summer thus far and that everything is well with you and yours. I'm calling about the Herez in my den, the one Oriental I didn't send out with you in May. Don't ask me how it happened, but there's a hole in the corner, and a pretty sizeable one at that. God knows I've tried to ignore it, but every time I sit down to read, there it is, big as life." She paused to take a breath and clear her throat. "Nothing urgent, Frank. Just stop by when you're in the neighborhood and work some of that magic of yours. I do love the rug and I don't want to see it get any worse than it already is. Whatever you can do to nurse it back to health will be graciously received on this end. Talk to you soon. Bye-bye."

Frank looked at the planner on his desk: every day for the next week read "Silberstein." Dipping his head and scratching the back of his neck, he penned in "Malloy" for Wednesday afternoon. He had no way of knowing how much work there would be that day, how far along he would be with the Heatherstone job, but at least now he had a reason to cut out early and visit with the amiable Janet Malloy.

There was a Plexiglas window in the office that allowed Frank to look out onto the warehouse floor. He got up from the desk and walked over to it. Billy and Kyle were rolling up the second shot of rug for Connie's master bedroom. With a black xylene marker, Billy wrote the rug's size on the white latex backing, then pulled up his shirt to wipe the sweat from his forehead. As he did this, Frank saw the smooth, hairless gut overhanging his waistline, a register in flesh of Billy's intemperance. He let down his shirt and stood for a moment with his back to the sun, staring open-mouthed into the recesses of the shop. His brow was heavy and there was a slight hunch to his shoulders, and the bags under his lightless eyes were droopy and yellow. The dull look on his face, which Frank had seen so many times before, was broken by a sudden fit of coughing. Billy hacked until his cheeks and nose turned crimson, and then spat a plug of phlegm into the street. If he didn't smoke so damn much and eat so damn much and drink so damn much, Frank thought, I might let him have this thing. He knows how to lay rug, but nobody ever taught him how to live.

Sporting a mangy white headband, Frank went out into the heat to supervise. He made sure that the cuts were straight, the sizes accurate, and the carpets rolled tightly and evenly. When they unfurled Alex Odondo's sisal, Frank operated the wheel. A 7-inch circular saw mounted vertically in a metal housing, the wheel had tiny rollers at its base and a black handle—fashioned after a bicycle grip—at the rear. Frank passed the wheel through the cross-hatched fiber, and a smell went up like singed hair. The sisal did not yield easily, forcing the saw to labor in sections until the devil's tendon lay split, raveled and hot to the touch.

As Frank was working, Billy took out a hacky sack and he and Kyle started kicking it around. Less than novices, they could only manage to keep it in the air for a few seconds at a time, and twice they booted the bag too high and hit the florescent light.

"You going to Bootlegger's tonight?" Kyle asked.

"Probably," said Billy.

"You taking me with you?"

"Not if you do what you did last time."

"That wasn't my fault. That was your fault. You should've never brought that dude out. He was high as shit already."

The hacky sack rolled over to where Frank was kneeling and he tossed it back to Kyle. With the bag in mid-air, Kyle tried to pass it to Billy but his sneaker got caught in the crotch of his shorts and he stumbled backward.

"Pull them up," said Billy, gathering the hacky sack.

Kyle hitched up his frayed white shorts, but they immediately slid down past his waist.

"What happened to the belt I gave you?"

"I forgot to wear it."

"Can he use some twine?" Billy asked Frank.

"No," said Frank, putting away the wheel. "The twine's for tying up rugs, not for Ricky Open Drawers." He pointed at the hacky sack. "And stop playing with that thing. You're making me nervous."

The three of them loaded the van with Monday's stretch of the job. Frank checked his supplies (pad staples, tackless stripping, carpet blades), and as he was throwing on an extra box of heavy-duty trash bags, he heard the exhaust fan in the rafters start to blow. This was a sign that it had become too hot for sane men to be working in the open air. Submitting, he wrote Billy and Kyle their checks and sent them home for the weekend.

FRANK HAD JUST FINISHED his bag lunch and was picking his teeth with the corner of a business card when Mr. Charleston's faded brown step van parked in front of the shop. Mr. Charleston was a flea marketer, and he drove an old Grumman Olson bread truck. He had painted the aluminum body with a roller and brush, and whenever Frank saw the van coming up the street, he thought it looked like a giant turd on wheels. From time to time, Mr. Charleston would swing by looking for remnants. On occasion he would ask Frank to bind them, and for these he would pay more. He sold them at flea markets all over the county, and swore they moved faster than any of his other wares—and he peddled everything from chandeliers to lawnmowers. In the beginning, Frank had found Mr. Charleston to be a low-balling huckster, but over the years he had grown to appreciate and even anticipate the arrival of this man in the poop-colored box. He was a bottom-feeder, but that meant he was always hungry.

Frank went outside and warmly shook Mr. Charleston's hand.

"I don't have anything for you," he shrugged.

"That's all right," Mr. Charleston replied. "I got something for *you* this time."

Mr. Charleston was a short black man with a shaved head. He kept his grizzled beard tight around the jowls and wore a small silver hoop in his left ear. He had on a long white T-shirt, oversized denim shorts, and loose-laced Timberlands that clopped when he walked. A clammy towel was draped over one shoulder, and with it he mopped his scalp and the pockets of sweat behind his ears.

"It's hot like the Ba*hamas*," he exclaimed, unlocking the double doors at the back of the van. Inside was a Salvation Army of random junk, a minor landfill of buckets, mirrors, lampshades, guitars—all piled on top of each other in a teetering sculpture of second-hand use. The smell was of things stored too long in a damp garage, what Frank's wife called "the moof," that mildewy odor to which all flea marketers are impervious.

"I was up at this big estate sale in Wynnefield," Mr. Charleston explained, "and I found this."

He dragged a rug from the bottom of the pile and spread it out on the street. It was a 4 × 6 Oriental, soiled at the fringes but otherwise in good condition. From its glossy cream field, short-cropped nap, and large rose medallion in cochineal red, Frank knew right away that it was a Kirman. Squatting over the rug, he separated the nap with his index fingers, noting a small loop where the warp and weft came together: the Sena knot. He brushed the face with his palm, first drawing it toward him, then drawing it away, and in either direction the wool retained its sheen.

"This is the real thing," he said.

"I *knew* there was something special about that rug," clapped Mr. Charleston. "The second I saw it layin' there in that woman's house, I knew it was quality. How old you think it is?"

"1920s, 1930s. Maybe earlier."

Mr. Charleston worried the fringe with the toe of his boot. "Know anybody who'd wanna buy it?"

"Not a lot of people want rugs like this anymore. Not even the rich. I might have a hard time moving it."

"I can sell it, no problem," said Mr. Charleston. "I just thought you might be able to get more for it. Them flea people, boy, they'll haggle with you over a bag of dog shit."

Since it was Mr. Charleston, and since the piece was a true find, Frank agreed to taking the rug and to a 50/50 split of the profits should he successfully broker a deal. He rolled up the Kirman, brushing off with a swipe of his pinkie the motes and crumbs hitchhiking on the back. Mr. Charleston whipped his towel in the direction of the shop and the grand stack of rugs for the Silberstein job.

"Looks like you got some work ahead of you," he said, his eyes glinting with the prospect of overage.

"Maybe a little too much," Frank said.

"*Too* much. Last month you were complaining about not having enough."

"Yeah, well, my uncle said to only take the good ones."

"Ain't that a good one?" Mr. Charleston asked, again whipping his towel.

"Good for the bank, bad for the bones." Frank said this with such philosophical authority that Mr. Charleston had no choice but to concur.

"You can retire afterwards," he said. "It'll be your legacy."

Thinking back to that morning and the house on Dunwoody Lane, Frank laughed quietly to himself. He didn't brood much upon his legacy, but he guessed that when Connie Silberstein's grandchildren ran through her many carpeted rooms, the name of Frank Renzetti would be light years from their lips.

"How much rug you think you put down in your life?" Mr. Charleston asked him.

"More than I care to remember."

"I bet if you took all that rug and laid it out end to end, you could make a ring around Saturn."

Frank smiled. "You think too highly of me."

Mr. Charleston hopped into his van and draped the towel over his head like a hood. "Find someone to buy that rug, and I'll think even higher."

He drove off and Frank walked back to the dry room to clean the Kirman. It was cooler here than in the warehouse proper, and quieter. He wouldn't be distracted by the phone ringing or the noise of cars passing on the street. A jumbled tower of cardboard carpet tubes stood in the corner, and to his right, always seemingly within reach, the homemade shelves where he stored brushes and sponges and towels and rags, erusticator, moth crystals, detergent, solvent—all the riches he had won during his many years as a tradesman. In truth, the dry room was a mess, dirty and disorganized, but Frank never saw it that way. He knew where everything was and where everything should be, and he had everything he needed here—

and much of what he thought he would never need—to bring a rug back to life.

He laid the Kirman on the cement floor and ran a vacuum cleaner over it, stopping short of the fringe so as not to catch it in the beater bar. Then he plugged in the rotary brush, first cousin of the janitor's buffer, and scrubbed the field deliberately, guiding the machine back and forth in slow, wide arcs, leaving swirls of shampoo as he worked downward from top to bottom. Next he turned on the steam cleaner, the primary appendage of which was a long metal wand tethered by vacuum hose and water line to a rumbling apparatus on wheels. As he drew out the foam, the rug's design—no longer obscured by lather—revealed itself. The dense cluster of leaves in the corners, known as boteh, were vigorous and dark, while the vines and trefoils along the edges were a pale, mint-green color. In places they traversed the border to mingle with the pink and red roses blossoming at the center. The prevailing cream landscape threw the attendant shapes and colors into sharp relief, making it appear more like a painting than a rug.

Shutting down the steam cleaner, Frank recalled his uncle saying that the Kirmanis were among the poorest weavers in Iran. He pictured them squatting at their looms, wiry villagers surrounded by bales of yarn, hand-tying each knot with clever, callused fingers. He took a long-handled comb with hard, plastic bristles from a hook on the wall and began stiffly raking the face of the carpet, lifting the pile in a single direction. Once the pile was of uniform height and there was no sign of divots, he lowered a wooden pole from the ceiling—one of the first things Frank had done after moving into the warehouse in Upper Darby was to install a mechanized pulley system for the dry room poles—and flapped the back of the Kirman over the long row of spikes. He tapped it down with the comb and raised it, slowly, evenly, to the rafters, giving the fringe a quick shake as it made its ascent. Frank switched on the oldest and the strongest of the Dayton floor fans and steered its gale upward. He watched the Kirman flapping in the vector of air, and couldn't decide whether it was a flag of conquest he was staring at or a flag of surrender.

CHAPTER THREE

"**H**ow is it?" Donna asked him.

They were sitting at the kitchen table, eating dinner. Donna had made white pizza with spinach and sun-dried tomatoes, and Frank was halfway through his first slice.

"It's good," he said.

"Does it seem bland to you?"

"It's white pizza. It's supposed to be bland."

"No it's not. It's supposed to be sauceless, not tasteless."

For years, the couple had ordered from the local pizzeria on Friday night, Pascilio's. Then, after a greasy pie had given her indigestion, Donna turned her back on Pascilio's and started making her own pizza. True to her tendency of overdoing things, she bought a recipe book, three basil plants, and a chrome-plated cooling rack. Just the week before, she had driven sixty miles for yeast. Frank was usually so hungry after work that he ate whatever she put in front of him, without questioning its origins. But two months into the Great Pizza Experiment, Donna's palate had become overly sensitive, and she had begun to doubt the quality of her weekly creations. The white pizza was something new.

Frank finished his slice and went for another, not because he liked the white pizza all that much, but because it was easier for him to eat the Experiment than it was to discuss it. "Did you talk to Paul?"

"He called when they got down there," said Donna. "They went to the beach after lunch. Francis didn't like the sand, but he liked the water."

Their son Paul was renting a beach house in Ventnor, a shore town just south of Atlantic City. Paul and his wife and their two-year-old son, Francis, had driven down that morning for a ten-day vacation, of which the last two days would be spent with the grandparents. Donna, who was madly in love with Francis, her only grandchild, had already begun packing and had twice been to the store for a new bathing suit. Though not as eager as his wife, Frank was looking forward to the trip. He hadn't seen his grandson in over a month, and he hadn't been to the beach in almost three years. After a week on the Silberstein job, he would be aching for the water and the company of his namesake.

"Maybe next Saturday I'll make them pizza," Donna said.

"Is Francis allowed to eat pizza?" asked Frank.

"If you cut it up into little pieces for him."

"They would have to be microscopic."

"Stop," she said. "That's how parents are these days. Cautious."

They finished their dinner and Donna began clearing the table. Frank took a drink of his beer and watched her. He thought that she was a picture of womanhood, full-bodied but not fat, seasoned but not old. He appreciated that Donna had never lobbied for plastic surgery, that all she had ever done to alter her appearance was a monthly dye-job at the salon. Rosy and hale, she needed nothing more than a hot shower and a few strokes of eyeliner to make herself ready for the world. A fine woman, a *good* woman—disagreeable at times, quick to flash the plastic at department stores, but she took care of him, and he took care of her, and this is how they survived in marriage, this is how they loved each other. Frank set down his beer and hooked the belt loop of her jean shorts, drawing her close. He rested his cheek on her breasts and linked his arms around her waist and squeezed, squeezed until she laughed and kissed the top of his head.

"You need a shower," she told him.

"I didn't even do that much today."

"It's the heat. All you have to do is go out in it."

"Then how come you don't smell?"

"I do," she said, helping him to his feet. "I'm just better at hiding it than you are."

On his way through the living room, Frank saw a big pile of cat vomit in the middle of the carpet. He closed his eyes and slowly shook his head. "Donna!"

"What?"

"Bring me some paper towels and the sponge."

Donna didn't ask why; there was enough of the persecuted in Frank's voice that she didn't have to. She brought him the paper towels and a sudsy blue sponge (she knew just the right amount of dish soap to use) and stood beside him as he bunched the paper towels into a mitt and scooped up the barf. It had a tan base the consistency of cottage cheese, with long veins of half-chewed grass circulating through it. Frank breathed heavily through his mouth, as few things were more nauseous to him than the odor of Ferdinand's puke.

"He must've just done it," said Donna in meek speculation.

Frank took the sponge from her and scrubbed the stain with a resigned diligence. "How long was he outside today?"

"Only a little while."

"I thought you said you weren't going to let him eat grass anymore."

"I did, but I read online that it's good for their digestion."

"Look in there," said Frank, and he thrust a finger at the wad of paper towels. "Does that look like it's good for the digestion?"

Donna backed away. "You don't have to be so nasty."

"Yes, I do," said Frank. "I feel like a janitor at a cat sanctuary. What's wrong with him?"

Frank handed Donna the sponge and paper towels and rose to his feet by a series of slow, weighted movements. He tried not to struggle in front of his wife; he tried to make it seem as fluid as possible, but when he straightened his back, exerting pressure on the root of his spine, he felt something—a quick volt of pain—in the back of his right leg. He moaned and reached down to massage the spot, just above his knee.

"What happened?" asked Donna. "You pull something?"

"I don't know what the hell I did." He leaned to one side, and continued vigorously rubbing his hamstring.

"If you pulled something, you need to see Dr. Temoyan."

Frank didn't want to see Dr. Temoyan. He had little use for doctors, and even less for chiropractors. For Frank,

pain was something that came and went, emerging suddenly and departing gradually, in the manner of all things
unwanted. His strategy of waiting it out, of working
around and through the pain, had been applied to almost
every part of his body, and it had never failed him, prov-
ing again and again that while patience is no silver bul-
let, it can immunize you to the virus of panic. Donna—the
names of medical practitioners always resting on the tip
of her tongue—thought differently, and it was under her
round, prescriptive stare that he angrily limped away.

"I'll make the appointment," she said. "I know how you
are."

After his shower, Frank went out to the back deck with
a bowl of vanilla ice cream and sat in the wicker lounge
chair that Donna had brought home the day before. It was
a creaky affair with striped vinyl cushions that clung to the
skin of his shirtless back. He intended to eat the ice cream
and find someplace else to sit, but then Donna came out to
water the flowers and he thought he had better stay put.

"What do you think of the chair?" she asked.

"It's nice," he lied.

"Not too stiff?"

"Nah. Just gotta break it in."

He lay with the bowl propped on his chest, and watched
his wife tote the watering can from daisy to vinca, ceramic
pot to hanging basket, sprinkling the soil, the leaves, the
blooms. He felt a cool bead of moisture roll down his stomach. A wren and some feisty sparrows pecked at the bird
feeder, and it was not long before the light around them
shrank and the hard lines of the world grew soft, and
Frank, sated from ice cream in a chair that needed him
more than he needed it, lapsed into sleep.

Hearing his snore, which was instantaneous, Donna took the bowl from his cupped hand and lit a citronella candle to ward off mosquitoes. She told herself that if Frank didn't come to bed before ten, she would go back out to wake him, but she fell asleep watching TV and never got the chance. Close to midnight, a persistent raccoon toppled the neighbor's trash can, and the ringing of metal brought Frank to. The candle had gone out, and a crescent moon flickered behind low, roving clouds. Frank sat upright and stared anxiously into the darkness. He often wondered why things seemed so monstrous when he woke in the middle of the night, how come ordinary objects like the picnic table now looked like a burnt Volkswagen. He knew that if he concentrated, the picnic table would normalize, but at this hour he was not willing to focus that hard.

He stood with his eyes half-shut, and the sound of the wicker chair releasing his body was like a hundred knuckles cracking at once. Frank somehow navigated the phantasmagoria of deck furniture and opened the sliding door. As he was stepping into the house, he felt and heard something peeling off his back, something he hadn't even known was there until it caught in the door frame and dropped to the ground. He turned and saw the striped vinyl cushion from the wicker chair. Out of an abiding hatred for pointless furniture (carpet installers have to move it twice, remember), he gave the cushion a good, hard kick. It skittered across the planks and got wedged beneath the deck's bottom rail—a parasite cast from the house of its host.

Donna had left the light on in the second-floor hallway. As he started up the stairs, Frank welcomed it, but nearing the top step, his right hand gripping the banister, his left flat against the wall, it seemed as though he were slaving under a stark, noonday sun. He attained the hallway and batted the light switch, drawing on that pot of anger already set to boil by the sly, stowaway cushion. Still not fully awake, Frank went into the bathroom to pee. The three beers he had drunk that night gave this particular evacuation an arc and a consistency he had long ago mourned the passing of. He belched victoriously and scratched a mosquito bite on his neck. He contemplated brushing his teeth, decided to wait until morning, and flushed.

In the bedroom, in the twitching light of the TV, Donna lay asleep on her side with her palms pressed together as if in prayer, the remote control sandwiched between them. Frank reached for it to turn off the set and Ferdinand, whom he had not seen curled up next to Donna, bit him on the pinkie. The bite didn't break the skin, but it hurt enough that Frank jerked his hand away and assumed a defensive posture. "I clean up your puke," Frank whispered, not wanting to wake up Donna, "and this is how you thank me." He stalked around to his side of the bed and Ferdinand hissed at him and shot out a paw. Frank stood motionless. The orange tabby looked at him in the heavy, chronically bored way that he always did, and settled back down to resume watching TV.

Most nights when Frank encountered Ferdinand loafing in his spot, he would gently lift him and place him on the floor. Ferdinand's departures were slow and saturnine, and Frank would feel bad for ejecting him, which is what the cat wanted. Eventually, Ferdinand would pad off to some other, less-contested part of house and no one would lose any sleep. Tonight, for whatever reason, the cat was not going to be removed by conventional means, and since Frank was hardly one for exotic feline enticement, he grabbed his pillow and headed for the guest room.

It took Frank over an hour to fall back to sleep. He lay in the narrow twin bed, listening to the intermittent chatter of the central air vent and staring at the two jade lions posing atop the dresser. They were bookends, and they belonged to his son, Paul, whose room this had once been. Whenever Paul came to visit, Frank would ask him to take the bookends home, along with all the other stuff he had left behind when he moved out: the clothes, the computer, the rack of dumbbells from his weight-lifting summer.

"Why don't you just leave it where it is," Paul had floated one Sunday before dinner. "It's not hurting anybody."

"I want to renovate the room," Frank had said, "and it'll be a whole lot easier with your things out of the way."

"What kind of renovation are you doing?"

They were talking in the living room while Francis stacked throw pillows on the floor, layering them according to a diagram that only he could see. Frank cheered each time Francis built a tower, and then cheered again when he ran into it and knocked it down.

"Paint and carpet," said Frank. "Nothing major."

"Don't you lay enough carpet at work? You have to come home and do it too?"

Paul finished his glass of Merlot and set it on the mantel. His voluminous brown hair shone with product and was combed and parted so severely that when Paul leaned forward Frank could see the white line of his scalp. He plucked a piece of fuzz from his shirt sleeve and blew it into the air. Francis watched his father do this and tracked the fluff as it drifted downward. It landed on the carpet, a little white pill, and he pounced on it.

"How much longer do you think you can do it?" Paul asked, frowning at his son playing with the fuzz.

"Until I can't do it anymore," said Frank.

"Your body has to be telling you that it's had enough. Do you ever listen to your body?"

"Only when it has something important to say."

"You should really start thinking about doing something else."

"What the hell else am I gonna do? I've been laying carpet for thirty-five years, as long as you've been alive."

"Just because you've been doing it forever doesn't mean you have to *keep* doing it. Have you ever thought about sales? You could work in the show room at General Floor."

"So I can stand around all day in khakis and a sweater vest? My body would definitely have something to say about that."

"That's not all you'd be doing. You're simplifying things."

"I've seen the guys at General Floor. They're a bunch of lum-lums."

"Then what about selling the business? You can spend more time with Mom, maybe get a shore house."

"Who am I gonna get to buy the business? I can't even find good help."

"You'd be surprised. There's people out there."

"From where you're at, maybe. But from where *I'm* at, there's nobody. It's just me."

"You made that choice, though."

"Yeah, because it was the only one I had."

Frank looked down at Francis in his black denim overalls and white Velcro sneakers. He was on his hands and knees, trying to make the fuzz disappear by mashing it into the carpet with his thumb. The fuzz kept rising to the surface and the boy couldn't figure out why.

"Leave that alone and get off the floor," Paul demanded, and he began picking up the pillows and arranging them on the couch.

Francis glanced at his father and then at his grandfather, and Frank clearly saw mischief in his eyes. As Paul was marshalling the last of the pillows, Francis located the fuzz and snuck it into his mouth. Frank knew that the rule book called for him to remove the choking hazard, but instead he sat there and watched Francis chew on it as if it were candy. He did not feel a sense of duty, nor did he feel any guilt, not even when Francis gulped hard and swallowed.

Frank rolled onto his back in the skinny bed and stared up at the long crack that divided the plaster ceiling. We are made to eat so much lint in this life, he thought, why not get a taste for it early. I gave Paul a taste, but he didn't like it. Spit it right out. He lives to ascend, a life without pain. But what about Francis? Maybe he likes it. Maybe it skipped Paul and he has it? Even so, his father would have him working in the circus before he'd let him crawl around on the floor with me. And who's to say he wouldn't be better off? Donna? The boy's mother? No, they'd all say the same thing: that's just not something you want to do for a living.

CHAPTER FOUR

Throwing open the side door of the van, Kyle gripped one of the heavy black tool boxes and lugged it up the walkway. His uncle carried the other tool box while Frank toted the broom and the radio. They moved slowly, solemnly, not attempting to hide their reluctance. Elaine George, who had seen the van backing up the driveway, met them in the foyer with a starchy smile and three pairs of booties. They were sky blue and made of a thin, papery material. They fit over the shoes and the elastic ankle band was supposed to keep them from sliding off, but it never did.

"Watch the finial on your way up," cautioned Elaine. "Vic just installed it this morning."

The finial was a topaz globe resting on a shiny brass base. Frank thought its milky swirl of gray and black hues made it look like an oversized marble. He touched it briefly, and for several moments afterward could not get over how cold it was, as if there were gel inside to keep its wintry feel.

Vic Satrapini was waiting for them in the master bedroom. He stood beneath the ceiling fan with just a few inches separating the blades from the top of his octagonal head. "What time do you think you're gonna be done?" he asked.

"Three-thirty, four o'clock," said Frank.

"I got the electrician coming at three to put recessed lights in the closet. Are you gonna be in his way?"

"Am *I* gonna be in *his* way?"

Vic stared at Frank, his eyes darkening, his brow peaking. "Yeah," he said, and his flabby mouth stayed open.

Frank knew that he was being sized up in this duel of indignation. He told himself to be patient, cordial. "I don't know," he said. "I guess we'll have to wait and find out."

The tension still in his face, Vic cocked back his head and nodded. He ran the tip of his tongue across his bottom lip, and this seemed to relax him. He looked down at the existing bedroom rug. "What do you do with the old?" he asked.

"Take it with us," said Billy, his arms loaded with shams.

"Good," said Vic, "'cause the dumpster's full." He pointed at Kyle's booties and snickered. "They look good on you."

He left the room and the floor shook with his every step. When he was out of earshot, Kyle asked, "How come *he* doesn't have to wear booties?"

"Because they couldn't find a pair to fit over his big fuckin' feet," said Frank.

He pulled the comforter and sheets from the king-sized bed, and all three of them tilted the mattress onto its side and pushed it into the bathroom. They leaned it against the shower enclosure, and twice it almost tipped over before they finally got it to stay. Going back for the box spring, they saw a dark object lying on the floor next to the nightstand. At first glance, Frank thought that it was a remote control, or maybe one of Norm Kershner's forgotten shoehorns. But when he drew closer, he saw that it was a flared 5-inch dildo in icy purple silicone. Billy and Kyle shared a lewd grin, but Frank stared worriedly at the prop, as if threatened by it.

"Was that there when we came in?" he asked.

"No," said Billy, "it must've just rolled out."

Frank scanned the room. "We need to hide it. At least until we're done. Then we can put it back."

As nonchalantly as one playing horseshoes, Billy picked up the dildo and flung it at his nephew. The instrument of pleasure split the air like a wobbly missile. Kyle let out a squeamish yelp and struck it down with a forehand smash. It bounced twice and then tumbled to a stop.

"I don't think I've ever seen him move that fast," said Frank.

"I should throw fake dicks at him more often," said Billy.

"She probably sticks that thing up her ass," said Kyle.

"You wanna see?" and Billy snatched the dildo and thrust it under Kyle's dodging nose. "What's the matter? Don't you know that Main Line shit don't stink?"

"Put it in the top drawer of the nightstand," said Frank, soberly enough to clip their antics. "And don't let me forget it's there."

Frank dismantled the rest of the bed, fighting its frame and headboard, while Billy and Kyle used plastic sliders to move the other pieces of furniture into the hallway. Between the chaise lounge, the slipper chairs, the window bench, and the nightstands, not to mention the chest of drawers, the ex-husband's high boy, and six different kinds of lamps, it took them a half-hour to clear the room completely. Customers have it in their heads that a carpet installer works with the furniture in the room, that he is gifted with the power of levitation and can suspend objects in mid-air as he goes about his labor. The truth is not in magic but in this prefatory bearing of loads. It is only after he has returned the room to its original, uninhabited state that the job can begin in earnest, only then does he feel he's ready to make the whole works go.

Billy and Frank sliced the old rug into three-foot-wide strips for Kyle to roll up and bring down to the van. Wall to wall they zipped, keeping their knives at a respectable distance, back and away from their legs. Obtuse yet ergonomic, the carpet knife looks like a small, blunt boomerang, more at home in the palm than its understudy, the boxcutter. A screw with a retractable, half-moon key opens and closes the knife on a swivel. The top and bottom pieces come apart like a pair of walking legs, and in the base of the latter is stored a six-deep stack of double-sided blades. When Frank's blade grew dull, he replaced it with a new one from the stack. Fresh blades come with a residue on their dark blue surface that is wet to the touch. This gives them a lethal sharpness. Frank didn't so much handle the new blade as defer to it, carefully slotting it in place at the head of the knife, leaving its upper half exposed like a slick, rectangular fin.

Beneath the rug was a cheap, urethane pad, the lemon-colored foam of the tract house. Most installers rip out the old pad and lay the new without bothering to pop any staples. It is not unusual to find two, sometimes three generations of staples embedded in a sub-floor. Ever his uncle's disciple, Frank would not allow himself to put the new pad down until all the previous staples had been extracted. As he pried up the first row of chisel points with a tuck knife, he invoked John's name and asked for deliverance from the installer before, or, as Frank's angry imagination dubbed him, the Carpet Ape. There were Apes in the other trades, butchers and hacks without standards or style, but none were as profligate as the one that haunted Frank's profession. His topped them all. The Carpet Ape was most brutal in his use of staples, discharging them in manic clusters across the plane of the pad.

"You anchor at the perimeter and at the seams," Frank said. "That's it."

"Guy must've had stock in the company," said Billy, quoting one of Frank's favorite lines.

The previous installer had driven the staples into the wood with such abandon that Frank had to pierce the grain with the tip of his tuck knife to unearth their crowns. It had probably taken the Carpet Ape just ten minutes to strafe the master bedroom; dislodging the bullets took more than an hour, and afterwards, as Frank sat on the denuded floor, watching Kyle sweep the staples into Billy's waiting dust pan, he thought about the beast. Had he ever stopped to consider the victims of his rage? Had he ever listened to the groans of the future? Had he ever felt the blister rising in his palm, red and raw as the sun? What kind of man *was* he?

Elaine had instructed them not to use any of the bathrooms in the house. The contractors were supposed to use the port-a-potty. *No* exceptions. Frank went outside and there was some poor mook in the blue box huffing and grunting and causing the thing to shake. Frank's bladder brimmed. He waited for a minute, but then the pressure became too much and he strode back into the house, that constant female sentry giving him away.

The plumber was still working in the powder room on the first floor, so that was off the table. Last he checked, Elaine and Vic were upstairs in the loft, talking about sky- lights. That meant the second floor was off-limits, too. He couldn't be sure, but he thought there might be a bath- room in the basement. He opened the door and walked quietly down the stairs.

The bathroom was at the end of a long hallway. Sneak- ing toward it, Frank became aware of a grinding noise, like something being churned or mixed. It was coming from the exercise room, which was adjacent to the bathroom. The door was half-open and Frank looked in just long enough to see Connie Silberstein riding a Stairmaster. She had her thick brown hair pulled back into a ponytail, and she wore a black vinyl tunic that looked like a trash bag. Sweat gushed from her scarlet face, as much from the workout as from the two space heaters blasting her from either side. She grabbed a water bottle and dumped its contents onto her head. She bent forward and the water drained off her nose and chin and splashed the base of the Stairmaster, parts of which had been eaten away by dark scabs of rust.

Frank peed as urgently as his prostate would allow, aiming his stream away from the water and leaving the bowl unflushed. He noticed nothing about the bathroom except for a copy of *Modern Dog* magazine in a wicker bas- ket by the toilet. With its petaloid ears and waxen fur, the pug on the cover could've easily been P.J.

He was halfway to the stairs when the grinding sud- denly stopped and Connie jumped into the hall. "You were told to use the port-a-potty," she yelled after him.

"There was somebody in it," Frank said. This was the

first time that he had ever spoken to Connie, the first time that he had ever seen her, in fact, and he could feel his mouth twisting into a nervous, apologetic smile. "I didn't know where else to go."

Connie peeled off her tunic, revealing a silver spandex tube top gone charcoal with sweat. She looked at Frank's feet and asked chippily, "Where are your booties?"

Fuck, thought Frank. *Fuck.*

"I took them off when I went outside," he said. "I'll put them back on when I go upstairs."

Connie edged closer to Frank, squinting at him with accusatory eyes. Her small bosom heaved inside its compact shell, and her breath came in short, whistling bursts through her nose. She blinked twice, and each time she made an odd gesture with her head, a kind of lunging, as if she were taunting Frank with her long, unevenly mascaraed lashes.

"Who *are* you?" she asked.

"I'm Frank Renzetti, the carpet installer."

He extended his hand and she shook it fiercely. "Did you already move the stuff out of my bedroom?"

"We did," said Frank, checking her face to see whether she too was thinking about the dildo.

"I guess that means I have to shower in Rachel's bathroom."

"Unless you want to wait until this afternoon," Frank joked.

"I'd rather not," she said with a heavy glare. "I have to bring the dog for his agility test at eleven."

Connie followed Frank upstairs and gathered some clothes from her chest of drawers. She didn't introduce herself to either Billy or Kyle, though she did ask Billy to get her a towel from the closet, and when he handed it to her she thanked him and smiled before strutting away.

"She doesn't seem so bad," Billy said, beaming like a bellhop who has just received a fifty-dollar tip.

After what Connie had done to him in the basement, harassing him over booties and the tinkling of desperate men, Frank wanted to smack Billy in the head for being so naïve.

"Go get the pad," he said gruffly, and struggled to fit on his booties.

The other crews' radios were set to the Squawker. Frank, who was never much for politics, tuned Windsor's to the classic rock station. Backed by the caterwaul of Robert Plant, they loaded their staple guns and began hammering the pad into place. Frank and Billy wielded a pair of newer, black-handled staplers; Kyle, urged by his uncle to try his hand at padding the closet, had to make due with Brownie, manufactured circa 1972, one of the oldest and most temperamental tools in Windsor's arsenal. If you didn't treat him just right, Brownie would show his age and lock up on you. Kyle didn't last five minutes before he swung too hard and jammed the antique.

"This thing is fucking *bull*shit," he cried.

"It's not the thing," said Frank, "it's the person holding it."

Kyle tried to unjam Brownie, but gave up quickly and called for his uncle.

"Just pick up scraps," said Billy, clearing the staple wedged in Brownie's mouth. "I'll finish the closet."

Kyle pushed his bangs behind his ears and loped around the room collecting bastard slivers of felt that had been shaved from the edges. One by one he dropped them into a trash bag, almost afraid to touch them. "I don't even care," he said, "this shit is mad itchy." He dusted the fibers from his hands and snapped the rubber bands on his wrists.

"You don't know what itchy is," said Frank.

He was thinking of the hair and jute pad that his uncle had made them use back in the 80s. The jute came from the linden tree, and the hair—the hair came from horses. Whenever Frank carried the pad, his forearms would break out in a rash, and the only way to soothe it was by running his skin under cold water. On hot, sweaty days, the filaments would settle in the crooks of his elbows, blackening the wrinkles there. They hung in the air like gnats; Frank would blow his nose and the tissue would be mottled with fuzz. He was forever scratching welts and picking motes from his eye, but John refused to switch pads because hair and jute was the industry standard. What Kyle was complaining about was 100% synthetic, 100% hypoallergenic. No longer endowed by the stables, it contained little to pique the skin or the sinuses, the outcome of thousands of hours of hard consumer science. That he was skeeved by it, then, made no sense to Frank, or, it made perfect sense. The kid was young; he hadn't yet suffered. Frank doubted there was anything in him willing *to* suffer—but there would be. Soon, we all have to carry the horse.

Kyle finished bagging up the excess felt and Frank and Billy went outside for the master bedroom's main shot of carpet, the 25-footer. The mid-morning heat was thick and moist: it felt like wading into batter. Vic, Elaine, and Connie were standing by the van's open back doors, inspecting the carpet.

Great, thought Frank, the inquisition.

They had pulled back the flap, and Elaine was holding a swatch of fabric against the field, explaining to Connie that once the chaise lounge and the slipper chairs were re-upholstered, the furniture and the floor would be in harmony, the whole room would come together as they had foreseen it.

"Trust me," she said. "You're going to wake up every morning and think you're still dreaming."

P.J. sat at Connie's feet, tethered by a short black leash. He turned his head very slowly and looked up at Frank and Billy. Stricken by the heat, all he could muster was one spiritless bark.

"Quiet," said Connie.

She yanked on his leash and threw such a torque on P.J.'s neck that he almost fell over. Billy, who was given to calling all animals "Buddy," offered the dog his hand to sniff. P.J. licked his fat, stubby fingers and the two slipped into reverie.

"Is this the right carpet?" Connie asked Frank, goading him with her clumpy lashes.

"Pink with purple polka dots, right?" he teased, but instead of a polite chuckle he was met with that same heavy glare.

"It seems a little darker than the sample," said Elaine. "I'll admit that."

"You're looking at it in the shade of the van," Frank said. "Anything's going to look dark in there. Excuse me."

Elaine and Connie stepped aside but Vic didn't move. His left hand was resting on the roof of the van and his right was jabbed into his hip. From atop his beefy totem, he peered down at the stack of carpet and shook his head to the bass notes of three contemptuous grunts. In them

Frank heard a dismissal, one man casually writing off another man's livelihood, and it came at an already sensitive moment in the carpet layer's day: right before he girds himself to bear the greatest load.

"Excuse me," Frank repeated, and this time Vic backed away, leaving behind a waft of scorched clove and Preferred Stock.

Stifling a cough, Frank took hold of the rug and pulled it toward him. With the roll halfway out of the van, he jacked it up onto his right shoulder and waited for Billy to do the same at the other end.

"Please be careful of the paint in the stairway," Elaine said. "They did the last coat on Friday."

"And don't you dare hit that finial," warned Connie.

"If you do," said Vic, "I'll come for you in your sleep."

As he neared the front door, his steps and Billy's in near-perfect unison, Frank heard Connie getting into her black Yukon, honking twice and driving away. He rejoiced at the sound, the temporary weakening of the hierarchy, one less asshole to answer to. Now if I could only get rid of the other two, he thought, stepping back into the coolness of the foyer, I might be able to breathe.

CHAPTER FIVE

The textured wool carpet that Elaine and Connie had chosen for the master bedroom was in the cut-and-loop style, with an arabesque pattern that repeated every two feet. It was the kind of rug you'd find in the pages of *Architectural Digest*, anchoring a sumptuously appointed room in a mythical house on the hill. Frank would have never put something like it in his own house, but he understood why people paid so much and waited so long to have it put in theirs. The rug was beautiful, it was well-made, and it would last forever. Even he couldn't deny that.

The walls had been painted sand dollar gray, and the colors in the rug were just as muted: beiges, whites, a few streaks of snuffed silver. Elaine George preferred a neutral backdrop, though some said her eye was too anemic. She believed that the blood was in the auxiliaries, in the paintings and pillows. Connie had argued with her over this. A conservative bedroom would only remind her of her ex-husband and the many safe choices he had made during their sixteen-year marriage. She wanted fiery reds and lusty oranges, a reclamation of verve, but Elaine talked her into a less libidinous palette, dominated by weightless colors like soft blue and dusty rose.

Connie worried that the room would end up looking like a nursery; crossing the threshold, she didn't want breastfeeding to be her first instinct. The more she fretted the more she needed to be counseled that everything— not just the master bedroom—would be perfect in the end. Tired of her beginning every other sentence with the phrase, "I just worry that . . . ," Elaine had given Connie a pencil, a ruler, and a stack of white copy paper. "Each time you feel a hair turning gray," she told her, "I want you to go to the planning center and graph." Elaine's therapist had recommended graphing as a way to sublimate negative energy, and the practice had done wonders for her over the years, helping her to slow down and focus her mind. After a dozen sheets of hand-drawn graph paper, Connie's kvetching went from hourly to daily, and she stopped texting Elaine at night ("I think I'm second-guessing the alternative to the brown leather club chairs," went one of the messages). Elaine considered this progress, and she praised Connie for not poopooing the idea and for creating such an authentic-looking product. The small, ruled squares in Connie's graph paper were indistinguishable from the real thing. In fact, her sublime grids were taped to the walls of the planning center, each with her initials flared in the corner to give them the stamp of art.

If Connie had stuck around long enough to watch Frank and Billy carry the 300-pound rug up the stairs, she wouldn't have felt a need to graph. The two men had done it so many times, neither spoke a single word of instruction to each other. On the landing, Frank turned around so that he was facing Billy, and then transferred the rug from his shoulder to his hands and lifted it high above his head. Billy responded by dropping the roll to just below his knees. With the woolen trunk at a forty-five degree angle, Frank walked backward toward the hall, and blindly ascended the last three steps. He stayed high, Billy stayed low, and the carpet hovered between them, bridging their flesh across twelve feet of massive, mutual appendage. In this way they cleared the landing without scraping the banister or the walls. Once Billy mounted the hall, they returned the carpet to their shoulders and proceeded into the bedroom.

At the count of three they let the rug fall to the floor, and its impact sent a tremor through the bones of the house. Frank drew a deep breath and touched his right earlobe. There was blood on his fingers when he took his hand away.

"What happened?" asked Kyle.

"Got scuffed," said Frank, wiping the blood on the seat of his shorts. "I didn't even feel it." He touched his earlobe again and looked at his fingers. "Better me than the walls."

He sent Billy and Kyle for the other, smaller roll of carpet and took a moment to study Connie's floor plan. The master bedroom was three feet wider than the goods. To make up the difference, Frank would have to seam an additional length of rug—known as the fill—to the main shot, and he would create this by joining at the head two 3' × 12' pieces. He tried to avoid head seams whenever he could (they always looked like hell), but in this case he had no choice. The room was just too damn long.

He unrolled the carpet with the grain running from the front of the house to the back. Then he got down on

his hands and knees and began to position the rug using
a kicker. Of all the carpet installer's tools, the knee kicker
is most synonymous with his profession. It's what comes
to mind when people think of him at his work, and what
they cite as the reason for his eventual knee replacement.
A dachshund hound in the abstract, the kicker has three
main parts: the head, the neck, and the rubber-cushioned
bumper pad. Inside the square-shaped head sit four rows
of metal teeth, and by turning a small dial on the head
these slanted spikes can be lengthened and shortened
depending on the thickness of the pile. Since this was a
cut and loop, about a half inch deep, Frank spun the dial
until the teeth protruded halfway beyond the base plate.
Still on all-fours, he extended the neck, planted the head
six inches from the baseboard, cocked back his knee,
and brought all 200 pounds of him to bear on the bumper pad. Frank was not a big man, but he was not a small
man either. The brawny mass at his core found focus in
the swift, hard ram of his knee, compelling the rug forward a good two feet in the length. He bumped the width
a few inches to the right and was satisfied.

Billy and Kyle brought in the other roll of carpet, and
from it they cut the two fill pieces. Frank unlatched a red
tool box and took out a straight-axle roller and a groove-
based seaming iron. He plugged in the iron and pushed
it aside to heat up. With a hand from Billy, Frank lay the
fill pieces end-to-end, adjusting them wherever the pattern failed to jibe, then tore off a strip of seaming tape and
slid it beneath the two flaps of rug. The surface of the six-
inch-wide tape was coated with a solid, meltable adhesive,
amber in color and waffle-like in texture. To guide the
amateur, a pair of solid blue lines was stitched down the

center. No passing, thought Frank whenever he paused to consider these lines. Stay in your lane.

The seaming iron began to smoke, a sign of readiness. Billy peeled back the corners of the fill pieces and Frank lifted the iron from its tray and placed it on the tape, keeping it there for ten seconds, allowing the heat to melt the glue before carefully moving the iron forward. Its curved black handle looked like the dorsal fin of some odd sea creature gliding through the water. The carpets dovetailed in its wake, though to give them a truer nexus, Frank tilled them with the roller, passing its spurred wheels back and forth over the seam until the pile was evenly compressed.

Waiting for the glue to harden, Frank located the pattern on the main shot and etched a line along its left side with a knurled poker. Sometimes the tip of the poker would catch in the loops, interrupting his flow, and like a musician who has lost his timing, Frank would have to lift the poker and start again. Following behind him, Billy ran a row cutter through the channel and separated the looping ribs. The blade inside the row cutter—an upright, isosceles tool—left a smooth, straight edge, and because it was a seam edge, Frank sealed it with a bead of fishy-smelling latex squeezed from a tall, white bottle held upside down, its nozzle pinched between thumb and forefinger. They mirrored these steps in prepping the fill piece, shook it into place, and, once they had matched up the pattern, nailed it to the floor in three strategic spots to keep it from walking. Kyle spooled out a long ribbon of seaming tape and they centered it beneath the two sealed edges and hooked it to the pins of the tackless at the perimeter.

Whenever he was confronted with a difficult task, one that required a high level of concentration and skill, Frank would ease the tension by whistling, usually something original, though at times he would draw on the hymns of his Catholic school youth, which gave the work a holy bent. For this seam, the longest he had seen in more than a year, Frank fell into a secular improvisation, inspired by the festoons that spread out before him in all directions. Uniting them carried with it a grave potential for error. A pattern as busy as this one could easily get away from you; the slightest shift could throw off the illusion, and he didn't have enough carpet for a do-over. A dry wall seam or a joining of wood can be disguised with caulk and paint. Not so with textiles. They forgive not. Frank had but one chance to get this right. If Elaine had to order more goods because of a less-than-perfect seam, he would be liable. Hence, the puckered lips.

"I'm gonna go get lunch," said Billy. "You want anything?"

"Yeah," said Frank, "a Chunky."

"What's a Chunky?" asked Kyle.

"It's a candy bar," said Frank.

"Do they still sell those?" Billy asked.

"Last time I checked."

"What if they don't have them?"

"Then don't get me anything."

Billy hung in the doorway, his arms at his sides. "I only have five dollars."

"Grab some ones out of my wallet," said Frank, inhaling the odor of paraffin wax given off by the melting glue. "It's in the van."

Frank resumed whistling after Billy and Kyle had left. Five dollars, he thought. Where does all his money go? Booze? Is he drinking *that* much? I don't pay him like I used to, but he should have more than five dollars in his pocket. The banks won't give him any plastic; cash is it for him. Cash and whatever else him and his nephew are using for currency these days.

The week before, Billy had asked Frank if he could borrow his credit card to buy a remote-control helicopter off the internet. Frank didn't even respond to him. He just sat there in silence, pretending not to have heard him. It's not that Frank wasn't charitable—far from it. He had leant Billy plenty of money over the years, for auto repairs, overdue bills, extra Christmas presents for his daughter, Vanessa, and never once had he asked to be repaid. But Frank's generosity wasn't boundless. In the spring, he had given Billy $150 toward a new washing machine, and—like a stunod—he lost the money the very next day. He said that he was roto-tilling his front yard and his wallet fell out of his pants. He didn't realize it until after dinner and spent the rest of the night sifting through loam with a metal rake and a flashlight. He never found the wallet, and claimed that his neighbor, a neo-Nazi, had stolen it while Billy was in the house. Since that cockamamie story, Frank had decided to refuse any solicitations of more than a few dollars. If Billy needed serious money, he would have to get it from someone who didn't know the first thing about him.

Frank was halfway through the seam; he had about twelve more feet to go. He glanced back at what he had already done. The seam looked good, better than he had expected, and to celebrate he pitched his whistling an octave higher. His uncle always said that a carpet man's expertise is measured in the quality of his seam. As fraught as the process could sometimes be, Frank rather enjoyed it. Seaming's hard-won legerdemain—the product of a life lived in feet and inches—brought him solitude, and with it a degree of control, a break from the turbulence of the world.

Ten minutes more and he was finished. He unplugged the iron and set it back on its tray to cool. From his tool pouch he took a small pair of nap shears and went down the length of the seam, trimming any stray tufts. He stood and scratched the elephant skin on both his knees. He walked over to the doorway and turned around as if he were about to enter the room. Closing his left eye, he held up his right forefinger and traced the arabesque as it traveled across the seam. He did this three times, but once would've been enough. The pattern in the main shot lined up exactly with the pattern in the fill. The naked eye couldn't tell that an extra piece had been added. Frank was pleased.

He ate his lunch in the van with the air conditioner on full blast. He had packed a ham and cheese sandwich, potato chips, a nectarine on the verge of ripeness, and a bottle of water. It had taken her almost three years, but Donna had finally succeeded in weaning him off soda, an admitted weakness. He hadn't touched a can of Coke in over six months, and was beginning to think that maybe he had put his addiction behind him. Yet on days like today he yearned for the sweet, sticky taste of it, that effervescent sting in his nose. It didn't help that Billy was sitting next to him swigging Fanta between bites of his hot dog. The bubbly orange liquid seemed to mock the clear, flat, tepid water Frank was now sipping. But Billy couldn't be faulted for this. It wasn't in his nature to be overly sensitive to the vices of other men; he had far too many of his own to gratify.

"Who told you they don't carry Chunky anymore?" Frank asked Billy.

"The cashier," said Kyle, who was sitting behind them on the floor of the van.

Billy nodded, his mustard-smeared mouth too jammed for him to talk.

Chunky was Frank's favorite candy bar, had been since he was a kid. He was disappointed when Billy had come back without one. He liked that Chunky was square-shaped, and that you could break it into quadrants if the spirit moved you. He also liked that it was made with raisins, something he felt more candy bars should add to their ingredient list, though he knew that nobody else shared his opinion. Frank understood that Chunky wasn't as popular as other candy bars (there were young people, like Kyle, who had never even heard of it), but he wasn't ready to accept that it might be endangered. Just the thought of it made him nostalgic.

"How much money did you take out of my wallet?" he asked.

"Two bucks," said Billy, using the hem of his shirt as a napkin.

"Then how come you only gave me one back?"

"Kyle needed a dollar for cigarettes. He was short."

For as long as Kyle had been coming into work with Billy, Frank had never once seen him eat lunch. He survived on Red Bull and cigarettes, the occasional French fry or scale of beef jerky leftover from his uncle. He didn't use a lot of energy, so he didn't need much fuel, but Frank often wondered how he made it through the day without crashing.

"You owe me a dollar," Frank said to Kyle. "I would take

it out of your pay, but I don't think you're gonna' make enough this week to cover it."

Giggling, Billy cracked the window and lit a cigarette. Kyle pulled up the catfight video on his phone and he and Billy huddled over the fractured screen, waiting for the carnage to begin. Frank recognized the look in both their eyes: he had seen it that morning when Connie's dildo had wound up on the floor. It was the beady gape of two young boys watching their first porno.

"You got five minutes," he told them, "and don't forget to leave the keys under the seat."

Vic had said that the electrician was coming at three, which gave Frank two hours to install the carpet, clean up, and move the furniture back into place. It was going to be tight, but Frank didn't want to ask for more time. Vic might get pissed and send the electrician in sooner. Frank thought it best to avoid any unnecessary exchanges with Vic, for fear of jeopardizing what little rapport he had with him. His opinion of the guy was low enough already, and he could sense that the feelings were mutual, though he wasn't sure why.

Upstairs, he grabbed the kicker by its neck and crawled to the far-left corner of the bedroom. Frank didn't wear protective kneepads: they were big and bulky, and the straps dug into his skin. Other guys in the trade lived and died by them, and Frank respected that. He didn't judge. He just couldn't tolerate wearing something that was only going to hinder his progress. The job itself was nothing but impediments. Why invite more? Donna said he was a macho fool for putting his knees at risk like that, and perhaps she was right, but until he was laid out on the surgeon's table, Frank would keep it raw.

He carved a thin strip from the top edge of the rug and tucked the flap into the channel between the tackless and the baseboard. This was a delicate process. If he cut too much, the carpet would be short, leaving a visible gap; if he cut too little, the carpet would be long, creating an air pocket beneath the surface. His depth perception had to be acute, the hand that gripped the knife strong and steady, able to pick up and follow the course of incision from one end of the room to the other. Luckily for Frank, the backing on Connie's rug was not too stiff with latex. As long as his cuts were true, he could expect a plumb finish all the way around.

This phase of the job kept Frank on all fours, his minor knuckles and heeled thumbs bearing much of the weight. Brought low, the carpet installer sees the room on a level unimagined by the resident. He becomes intimate with its forgotten parts, its cable wires and outlets, doorstops and registers. Things present themselves beneath the baseboard: pennies, Q-tips, stamps, Legos. Never anything of value, but then he's not in the capacity of an explorer, he's not down there to make discoveries. Prostrate before this netherworld of which all but the toes are ignorant, he thinks of himself as a caretaker of the invisible, warden of the dark and dusty corner. The thought brings him neither pride nor honor, just a deeper sense of the mission to leave things as he found them, to act as if he—like the forgotten—were never even there.

Frank polished off the bedroom in less than an hour. Not a record-breaking time, but a good one considering the room's dimensions. The closet's valet table was giving Billy some trouble, so Frank went in to give him a hand. There was a pair of red leather pumps on the ground, a casualty of Billy trying to maneuver the rug around the table. Frank picked them up and looked for the empty space in Connie's vault. Again he was awed by its museum quality, the sacred science of its sprawling array, but his wonder quickly devolved, first into quizzical disgust (Where the hell is she going with all these shoes?), and then into a stabbing, legitimate dread (What if she knows they've been moved? What if she knows they fell?). Though Connie hadn't specifically warned him about the shoes, Frank felt that any discrepancy in their display, down to the most infinitesimal disturbance, would not be overlooked, and could lead to more pressure, more scrutiny. Therefore, he took the shoes by their studded ankle straps, one in each hand so they wouldn't rub together, and held them up to the light, inspecting them for damage.

"Like them, do you?" said a woman's voice.

Frank froze, then, still holding up the pumps, light pinging off the studs, he turned and saw Gildea the housekeeper standing behind him with a laundry basket full of clean towels. Her reddish-brown hair was combed to one side and her cheeks were heavy with rouge. The tan scrubs she wore hung loosely on her streamlined body, betraying no curves. She had on petite, white canvas bobos with only three eyelets to a side.

"They got knocked down," said Frank. "I'm just seeing if they're all right."

Gildea set the laundry basket on the valet table and gestured for Frank to give her the shoes. There was something both mild and serious in her manner, as though she didn't care whether the shoes were damaged, only that *she* be allowed to examine them.

"Valentino Garavani," she said. "Haven't seen her wear

these in months." She gave the pumps a once-over and popped them back into their slot.

"Will she know?" Frank asked.

"Probably. You can't even hide what you didn't do from her."

Frank looked up at the collection. "This must've taken her a long time to put together."

The housekeeper smiled. "It would've, if she'd been the one to do it."

The Irishwoman soughed off with her basket, and, watching her go, Frank felt a kinship with her, a peasant's union. Here was an ally, someone who understood, someone he could trust. He was glad to have her on his side. Because of its unexpectedness, the feeling stayed longer in his heart, getting him through the closet despite his fatigue. To atone for having knocked down the shoes, Billy did the brunt of the kicking and tucking, and Kyle, in a surprise turn, vacuumed the master bedroom without having to be told. The rolling din of the Sanitaire soothed Frank, for it was a sign of the day's coming end. But as soon as Kyle switched off the vacuum, Frank heard several people walking up the steps. They were all talking at once in a mish-mash of voices, some belonging to adults, others to children. Elaine George's was distinct among them, as was Connie's petulant valve. They were coming Frank's way—to inspect, to enquire, to preempt his little peace. He rose to meet them in the bedroom.

Connie and Vic stood on one side of the doorway and Elaine stood on the other side. Home from day camp, Connie's two daughters—Miranda and Rachel—stayed in the hallway, scared to walk on the brand-new carpet. Miranda was tall and rangy with copper-colored hair that lay in a thick braid over her shoulder. The black violin case she carried gave her an air of refinement, though her moody eyes and grim-set mouth worked hard to spoil the distinction. Her younger sister, in whose arms sat the intractable P.J., was in higher spirits. She rocked the dog back and forth like a baby, letting him lick the sweat from her sun-blotched cheeks.

"I like the rug," she said definitively. "It's fancy." She smiled when she said "fancy," exposing a mouthful of neon pink braces.

"It looks great," said Elaine. She turned to Connie. "What do you think? Do you love it?"

Connie walked slowly across the room, her head on a swivel. "I can see the seam," she said. "Am I supposed to?"

"No seam is 100% invisible," said Frank, "but this one's pretty close. Nine out of ten people are gonna walk in here and not notice it. I guarantee you."

"Well, I guess I'm that one person," said Connie, "because I can see it." Her small, pointy face became flushed and sweaty. "Every morning when I get out of bed, I'm going to see it."

"Don't look down," kidded Vic.

"How can I not? When I put on my slippers, my eyes naturally go there."

Frank pointed at the bare windows facing north and west, through which the mid-afternoon sun was shafting. "You're getting a lot of glare," he said. "Once your window treatments are up, it shouldn't be an issue."

"And the bed's going to cover some of it," reasoned Elaine. "That's why we decided to put the seam there, because the bed goes up against the far wall."

"What if she doesn't want the bed over there?" said Vic.

"What if she changed her mind and wants it over here now?" He spread his burly arms, almost spanning the wall behind him. At this posturing, Miranda rolled her eyes and struck off down the hallway toward her room.

"Before we start rearranging the floor plan," said Elaine, "let's just see what the carpet looks like with all the furniture back in the room."

Frank, Billy, and Kyle began arranging the furniture per Elaine's directives. They started with the bed, which Frank recalled being much lighter at nine o'clock that morning. They fought the mattress onto the box spring, and then for five minutes tried to center the bed between the windows, using quick jerks of the pelvis to jockey it. Each time that Frank nudged it one inch to the left, Elaine would ask Billy to nudge it one inch to the right. Connie stood beside her, stating more than once, "The comforter's not going to match the carpet," as if repeating herself would somehow solve the problem. All the time they were fooling with the bed, Frank kept glancing over at Connie, but nothing in her expression said to him, "Dildo." Maybe she forgot she put it under there, he thought. It did look pretty old. Or maybe she has more than one of them stashed and she lost track of it. They could be hidden all over the place like Easter eggs. Christ.

"Can I put the dog down?" Rachel asked. "He's getting heavy."

"You can put him down," said Connie. "Just don't let him come in here."

"I won't," said Rachel.

To no one's surprise, P.J. went straight for the master bedroom the second his paws touched the floor. Like a sentinel, Vic was first to catch him peeking inside the door. He called P.J. a "shitass" and frightened him back into the hallway with a stamp of his boot.

"Don't be mean to him," said Rachel, squatting next to P.J. and scratching him under the chin. "He's sad because he failed his agility test."

"Why don't you take him for a walk?" Elaine suggested.

"It's too hot," Rachel said. "He'll get heat stroke."

Twice Frank had to ask Rachel to move, and twice she complied, coaxing P.J. by his collar and murmuring secret verses in his ear. Rachel didn't care that he had a bad reputation, or that his sacs were enflamed, or that he couldn't jump over a broomstick. She loved him anyway. Her fondness for the pug made Frank think of Donna's relationship with Ferdinand. Every time the animal did wrong, their bond grew stronger. This must be rare in the world. Under no other circumstances would throwing up on the carpet win you a seat beside the queen—and the king's seat at that. Frank was not a lover of animals; he had to continually find new ways to endure them. He couldn't understand why they were given such a wide margin for error, and why their prancing in oblivion was often met with pity rather than punishment. Maybe it's because they're Modern Pets, he thought. If your face is on the cover of a magazine, people will let you run wild. Like rock stars trashing hotel rooms, it's all part of their celebrity.

"I'm hungry," Rachel whined. "What are we having for dinner?"

"I'm not thinking about that right now," said Connie shortly. "If you're hungry, go downstairs and get a snack."

"We don't *have* any snacks," Rachel said. "The men ate the rest of the Party Mix."

"There's a new one in the pantry," said Vic.

Rachel's face drooped doubtfully; a skeptical P.J. barked. "I bought it this morning," said Vic. "I swear."

Rachel led P.J. down the stairs. The electrician and his apprentice were coming the other way, a half hour later than expected. They spread a drop cloth in the closet and got to work on the lights. Except for the apprentice making a few trips to the van for parts, they stayed out of Frank's way. It always made him uneasy when contractors swooped in just after he had finished, his handiwork too green to even be christened. He found it disrespectful, but he knew that they couldn't be blamed for it, at least not fully. They were subject to the same whims of scheduling as he was. And in a house like this one, where people seemed to be watching and waiting in every possible corner, you couldn't expect your work to remain pristine for too long.

Connie and Elaine went around making slight adjustments to the furniture: pushing the window bench closer to the wall, cheating the nightstands away from the bed. Elaine carried with her a small tape measure, and each time they placed something she would measure its distance from both the wall and the nearest solid body. She even did this with the lamps and knick-knacks. In staging the décor, one-sixteenth of an inch mattered greatly to Elaine, the space between just as important as the space inhabited, wind no less vital than water.

Because it was casting a shadow on the light switch by the door, Elaine persuaded Vic to help her move the high boy. "Just enough to show the face plate," she said. Anyone could see that the high boy was top-heavy, its cabriole legs skinny and brittle. Rather than lift it off the ground and walk it over two inches, they forced it from the side.

The front right leg buckled and squealed, and before they realized what they were doing, they had almost snapped it clear off. Elaine jumped back and clapped her hand over her mouth when she saw the splintered leg, while Vic stared at it like a man with a shotgun about to put down a horse.

"That was *Norm's*," said Connie. The name of her ex-husband dropped from her lips like a once-chewed bite of mealy apple. "You can break all four legs if you want. I don't give a shit."

"But it's such a nice piece," said Elaine. "When the Amish come to shave off the burl, I'll have them look at it. Maybe they can fix it."

"When are they coming to do that?" Vic asked.

"Wednesday," said Connie. "And don't have them look at it. Have them throw it out."

"Do any of you guys want it?" Elaine asked Frank and Billy.

"Sure, I'll take it," said Billy excitedly.

For the second time that day, Frank wanted to smack Billy in the head. After all the work they'd done, he was going to add to it by schlepping another man's piece of hobbled furniture out to the van. "You and Kyle can take care of that," Frank said. A voice warned him against giving Kyle that much responsibility, but another voice, the voice of his body, told him to stay where he was, let the kid's muscles quake, yours have done their share.

Billy and Kyle took the high boy away and Vic stepped into the space left behind. "Do you have something else to put here?" he asked.

Turning to Elaine, Connie said, "I want to do the porcelain cabbage on the stand."

"Too skinny," said Elaine. "You need mass."

Vic's cell phone rang and he ducked out to answer it. The electrician called Elaine into the closet, and, instinctively, Connie followed her. Standing there alone, Frank knew what he had to do. He remembered which nightstand it was by the zig-zag scratch on the face of the drawer. He opened it and without hesitation plucked the dildo from atop a swell of junk that briefly reminded him of Mr. Charleston's step van. The dildo was heavy in his hand, solid. As he rushed around to the other side of the bed, the side from which he believed it had fallen, he shielded it with his body, holding it vertically against his chest. He knelt beside the bed and found a spot between the box spring and mattress and stuffed it in. He propped up the mattress to see if he'd gone too far, or not far enough. In the light from the window, the dildo looked like a tiny animal retreating into its burrow, happy and thankful to be home.

CHAPTER SIX

The renovation of Connie Silberstein's house had begun the previous spring, and since then her neighbors had lodged several complaints with the zoning board about the pace and scope of the project. They made phone calls and wrote e-mails and one impassioned Heatherstonian even drove to the township building to arraign the commissioner in person. They complained about the overflowing dumpster and the rusty scaffolding on the side of the house that had never been broken down. They complained about the noise—of the table saws, the nail guns, the compressors, the radios. They complained about the ugly, stank, fly-infested port-a-potty that no one ever came to pick up. But mostly they complained about the fleet of work vans that was always parked on their street. "How many people does she have working in that house?" they demanded. "Isn't there a limit to the number of contractors allowed on the property at one time? We can't pull out of our driveways anymore. We can't even *see* the street, let alone drive down it."

On Tuesday morning, as Frank was turning onto Dunwoody Lane, he saw Connie's next-door neighbor—an older woman sporting headphones and a pink visor—power-walking in the middle of the street, the eternal, blue-collar tailgate sprawled out behind her. When she got within twenty yards of the van, she drew her forearms close to her chest and pumped them up and down like pistons. Frank beeped at the woman, but she did not slacken, she did not yield. She sent the pistons into overdrive, and her eyes shone like high beams in a midnight game of chicken.

Frank slowed down and swung the van to the right, almost clipping the woman's shoulder with his side-view mirror. She threw back her head in triumphant disdain, yelled something inaudible over the radio, and gave the flank of the van a reverberating smack, as if to scold it for trespassing. Frank jammed the brakes and got out and stood by the open door with his lips parted in mild astonishment. He waited for the woman to turn around and face him, to acknowledge what she had done, but she continued walking in a straight line, the cicadas saluting her from their garrets in the trees. He went back to where she had spanked the van and there was a slender handprint in the black coat of grime.

Kyle hung his head out the door. "Bitch!" he yelled.

"Yo!" snapped Frank. "Nobody needs to hear from you."

"Is it dented?" Kyle asked.

"No," said Frank, running his finger through the dirt, "it's filthy."

Today they were installing Alex Odondo's sisal on the main stairs and in the second-floor hallway. Billy and Kyle volunteered to remove the contoured rug from the hall; Frank, working alone as he preferred, tore up the old stair runner. It had been applied using the capping method. Here, the carpet is molded around the nose of the step and affixed with a row of divergent point staples. If the nap is dense enough to hide the impressions of the staples, and the installer metes out the bullets from his tacker, capping results in a clean, upholstered finish. Low-cut and thin of field, Connie's runner should not have been capped. The Carpet Ape—that anonymous conductor of pogroms— had come at these stairs with but one urge: to annihilate them. Now it fell to Frank to build them back up again, to do right by them.

He loosely folded the runner with the staples on the inside. Then he ripped the foam pads off the steps and stacked them by the front door. His leg had begun acting up (a dull ache in the back of his thigh that wouldn't go away), so he sat on the bottom step and watched the plumber working beneath the powder room sink. He was tightening the nuts on the S-trap with a cast-iron pipe wrench, and because of the odd angle at which his body was tilted, the Phillies hat he wore slipped off his bald head and landed in the toilet. As if nothing out of the ordinary had happened, the plumber finished tightening the slip nuts and ran the faucet on high to test for any leaks (there were none). Even then, he dabbed his brow with a handkerchief and sipped his cup of coffee before bending over the john and sticking his hand into the bowl. He lifted out the hat and held it by the snap-back as a runnel of water drained off the brim.

"Doesn't that hat know you're not allowed to piss in the house?" Frank said.

The plumber looked at him and smiled. "The one good thing about this line of work," he said, rinsing the hat in the sink and hanging it from a silver towel hook, "you never have to go too far to take a leak."

He came out into the foyer and shook Frank's hand. His name was Bruce Patton, and he was a few years older than Frank. He had broad, furry arms corded with muscle, and wore old-fashioned suspenders to keep his Dickies afloat. He told Frank that he had been on the Silberstein job since April, and didn't expect to be out of there until the first week of September. "After three months, I'm still waitin' on parts and fixtures," he said. "Instead of ordering what I need, they're puttin' a rush on shit like this." He flicked the finial, and his nail made a toneless pop against the cold glass ball. "This thing costs more than a used car. Would you put anything this ugly in your house?"

"Not if I didn't have to," said Frank. "And even if I did, I wouldn't be able to afford it."

"That's what it is with these people. They don't have to do *any* of this shit. They do it because they *can*."

"Money to burn."

"At least until the alimony runs out."

"Is that where it's coming from?"

"It's gotta be. Her ex-husband's a big-shot lawyer."

"Obviously not a divorce lawyer," said Frank, and the two men were quiet as they chewed on this for a spell.

"How do you like Vic?" Frank asked.

"I like that he pays on time," said Bruce.

"Yeah, well, he's not the one payin' me."

"Has he been giving you shit?"

"A little."

"I'll tell you what I tell everybody: He's not trying to make your life miserable; he just enjoys giving people bad news."

"Aren't they the same thing?"

"Maybe, but that could be why he's picking on you. You think it's about you, when it's really about him."

"It's about the work," said Frank, "which is hard enough already without him reminding me of it every time I see him."

"Yeah," said Bruce, overcome by a sudden weariness, "it's always been about that."

He squeezed his right shoulder and winced, then he flapped his arm a few times and pressed on his shoulder again. He told Frank that he had had surgery last year to repair a torn rotator cuff. He claimed it was the worst decision he had ever made. The doctors used plastic rivets to reattach the tendon to the bone, and every time he moved his shoulder, he could feel them traveling around in there, pinching and crunching. The procedure was meant to reduce his pain level and give him a wider range of flexibility, but his "tator," as he referred to it, had only gotten worse since the surgery, and now the doctors were telling him that he would have to have the anchors removed.

"Loose bodies," he said with a smirk. "That's what they called them. 'We have to go in and retrieve the loose bodies. They've become dislodged.'"

"How big are they?" Frank asked.

"About the size of a machine screw," said Bruce, and he held up his thumb and forefinger with a slight space in between. "They said they would never need to come out. I say they never should've gone in. But what do I know? I'm just a plumber."

Frank almost brought up the pain in his leg as a comparative study, but he decided not to, partly because he didn't want to compete with Bruce's war story, and partly because he feared that describing his problem would somehow legitimize it, would, as in an act of conjuring, make it more real.

"Maybe it's a good thing," said Bruce, "the surgery not taking. What did Roberto Duran say in that fight?"

"No mas."

"No mas. I'm broken and I can't be fixed. Let me go sit in the corner."

"To do what?"

Bruce made like he was going to punch the finial. "Not get hit."

They both heard a fuss in the kitchen. The tile-layer screamed at P.J. for drinking from his slurry bucket and chased him into the foyer, bellowing, "Next time I *drown* you in it." His black muzzle stained from the khaki-colored water, the dog chugged past Frank and took refuge with the plumber.

"These young guys," said Bruce, "they sure let you know when they're pissed."

As the dog circled Bruce's feet, Frank saw the irritated sacs on either side of his high-held ass; they looked like a pair of red, squinty eyes. He asked Bruce if anything could be done about the dog's scooting, and the plumber said, "Yeah, keep him locked up with me all day long," and he whistled for P.J. to follow him into the powder room. "But," he added drily, "that probably won't happen."

Frank went upstairs—where Billy and Kyle were almost through—and poked his head into the master bedroom. He ignored the new set of silk shams arrayed on the bed, and the porcelain cabbage that Connie had fought—and finally won—to replace Norm's high boy. He looked only at the seam, and just like yesterday before lunch, when he had stood in the very same spot he was standing in now, he could not see the junction. He knew it was there, of course, but to the casual eye of the houseguest it would be undetectable. And that's who Connie was trying to impress: houseguests. Did she think they were going to drop to the floor and sniff out the seam? Didn't she know that most people notice a rug only when it's missing? A rug is like a tree in this respect: it becomes apparent in its absence. When a rug is down, it's the equivalent of white noise, dwelling on the fringes of perception. Few are those who consciously acknowledge its presence, who pause to appreciate even a new carpet. Connie was not yet unconscious, but in time she too would forget. A judge as fanatical as her would rise one morning to put on her slippers and find that the world wasn't crashing down around her. But the price of her eventual happiness would not be Frank's immediate misery. No—he stood by his work.

Around mid-morning, Frank cleared a space in the corner of the garage and here they brought the sisal and the tapestry binder. One of the overhead doors had been left open to foot traffic, which meant relief from the sun but not from the heat. Billy unrolled Connie's new stair runner: the decorticated sisal was flaxen in color, with two cords in the warp and three in the weft. To off-set the blondness, Connie and Elaine had chosen a brown cotton binding. From a large reel, Billy snipped two lengths of binding and lay them on either side of the runner. Then he set about cutting new felt pads for the steps.

An old refrigerator stood by the open garage door, and stuck to its face was a cluster of multi-colored alphabet magnets. Kyle bobbed over and spelled out "PERCMAN" and took a picture of it with his phone. He looked at the picture and then readjusted the letters, straightening the "M," compressing the "R" and the "C." He took another picture and seemed to like this one better.

"Hey, Percman," said Frank, lifting the binder from its wooden case, "cut me 28 pieces of tackless at 31 inches."

"Where's the tackless?" Kyle asked.

"In the van," said Frank, "where it always is."

Kyle flicked the rubber bands on his wrists and blew a long jet of air through his bangs. He looked out into the fervent sunlight and mewled just loud enough for Frank to hear.

"Move!" he commanded. "You're a nickel holding up a quarter!"

Boxier than a sewing machine, the tapestry binder weighed 55 pounds, ran on a 220-volt motor, and was rigged with a diamond-point, titanium-coated needle. Frank clicked a fresh bobbin into the shuttle case and threaded the needle by gently squeezing the trigger switch. He attached the binding to both sides of the runner using a straight blind stitch. The machine felt and sounded good: there was a humming ease to the action, a clarity and flow. He stopped to wipe the pellets of sweat dripping off his nose, then flipped the sisal onto its face and smeared latex along the right and left edges. As soon as the glue became tacky, he made taut the flaps of binding and pressed on them until he was sure they had stuck. After giving the latex a few more minutes to cure, he rolled up the runner and carried it into the house.

Billy had padded the steps and was hammering the last few strips of tackless into position on the risers and treads. A customer had once said to Frank, "There is no uglier thing in life than tackless stripping," and he had agreed with the woman. Despite its value to the trade (it revolutionized wall-to-wall carpeting, eliminating the need for tacks in securing a rug's perimeter, hence the name "tackless"), there had always been something punitive in its construction. The sharp, closely staggered pins can tear at the flesh if tackless is handled in haste. Just pulling it out of the box has the potential to inflict harm, so the installer develops a healthy fear of the stuff. Customers share his fear, though theirs tends toward the superstitious and phobic. They make tackless out to be some kind of sleeping menace, an underground network of identical torture devices that will someday achieve consciousness, unnail itself from the floor, and rise up to mutilate their children. The same woman who had declared tackless utterly grotesque forbid her five-year-old son from playing too close to the walls of his bedroom—or any room for that matter. She worried that the pins would breach the nap and stab his little toes.

The manner in which Billy was applying the strips did nothing but feed that anguish. The first piece was nailed near the back of the tread, with the pins facing inward; the second piece was nailed by the bottom of the riser, the pins pointing downward. A finger's-width gap between the pins gave the impression of a chomping maw, as if each step had its own set of recessed fangs. Vicious—even to jaded eyes. But the finish that Elaine wanted could not be produced otherwise, for she had requested a waterfall, and the cascade would not flow correctly unless it fell into the jaws of those wood-and-metal piranha.

"Bring in the sisal for the hall and scribe it out," Frank told Billy. "And make sure you have tools up there. I don't want you walking up and down a thousand times while I'm on these stairs."

Once they had carried in the hallway shot, Billy and Kyle stayed on the second floor, out of Frank's way, and

for a solid twenty minutes he had the stairwell to himself. Space, authority, rhythm, calm. Tools like toys in
his hands, Odondo's sisal friendlier than most. The work
coming easy, thoughtless, graceful. Inhabiting him and he
it. But then the parade started, as it must always. First the
electrician and his apprentice walked up the steps, then
the painters, then the carpenter. And they didn't do this
just once. They ascended and descended repeatedly, and
each time somebody marched by, Frank would have to
stop what he was doing and let them through. The men
weren't being disrespectful; they had a job to do. They said
things like, "My bad," and, "Last time, I promise." Frank
recognized their apologies with a lipless nod, but his hammer rebelled, swung in cresting rage. He whaled upon the
chisel, driving the carpet deep into the jagged mouths,
and the lights in the foyer trembled, and the piqued ears
of Connie's neighbors heard the vengeful clang. At last
Frank said to the carpenter, "Is there any way you guys
can use the back stairs?" The carpenter, who left wood
shavings behind him like a trail of breadcrumbs, replied,
"We would, but the hardwood floor guys are re-staining
them." And for a few thwacks the faces of the hardwood
floor guys were projected on the head of Frank's chisel,
soon replaced by other, more deserving faces—Connie's,
Vic's, Elaine's, and when they had been obliterated, he
took the storm to the house itself, his every strike a boom-
ing chastisement. He lay into the joists and studs, the
walls and windows, retaliating against the house's dumb
silence, cursing it, finally, for ever having been built.

FRANK TOOK HIS LUNCH in the van, as he had done the
day before. Billy and Kyle remained inside to finish scrib-

ing; neither had money to buy lunch, and after what had happened yesterday, Frank wasn't feeling too generous. His lunch was identical to yesterday's, but the appetite he had worked up installing the runner brought novelty to the sandwich, the chips, the fruit. He ate the nectarine down to the pit, and sucked it clean before spitting it into the foil from his sandwich. A drowsiness came over him. He reclined in his seat and napped indulgently.

He was awakened by three sharp knocks on the window. Vic was staring at him from the other side of the glass. Frank rolled the window down and the heat poured in like sauce.

"You weren't supposed to put the runner down until Connie and Elaine got home from the marketplace," said Vic. "They wanted to see how it looked with the binding."

"Nobody told me," said Frank.

"Elaine didn't call you?"

Frank's flip phone was on the dashboard, where it had been cooking since early that morning. The black leather case was hot to the touch. He opened the phone and saw that there were two missed calls from Elaine.

"You need to keep that with you," said Vic. "It's not doing you any good in there."

"They're not even back yet," Frank said. "Waiting would've put me a half-day behind. I'm trying to get out of here at some point."

"You've only been here a day. Don't be so eager to leave. It'll make you sleepy."

Vic winked at Frank and gave him a lopsided smile as he turned toward the house.

Son of a bitch doesn't even ask you how you're doing, thought Frank. He just starts right in with it. And what does he think I'm going to do if they don't like the bind-ing: take up the runner? After I just killed myself put-ting it in? And why wouldn't they like the binding? *They* picked it. For *three months* they picked it. How do you sec-ond-guess something that took you three months to pick out? Are you *that* fucking paranoid? I know it's the first thing you see when you walk in the house, but come the fuck on already!

Frank pissed in the airless port-a-potty, breathing through his mouth to avoid the reek, and went back to the garage. Billy was binding the hallway sisal, which had the general shape of a long-barreled handgun. Kyle stood off to the side, hands in his pockets, trying to stay awake. Frank trusted Billy with the tapestry binder; he and the machine had a rapport, a kind of pact to never do the other wrong. Frank would readily admit that Billy had him beat when it came to binding, though he still did the majority of it himself, because customers expected him to, and because Billy did not present the appearance of mastery, not in his bearing or his speech or his wardrobe. The neckline of every single one of his T-shirts devastated by stretching, he looked for all the world like a schlub, and schlubs do not inspire confidence. He would never be an Ace (Frank knew this, Billy himself knew this), but he offered occa-sional flashes when the binder was in his hand.

From a leftover hunk of sisal, Frank cut three 2' × 4' throw rugs for Billy to bind. Connie would use them in the foyer; sisal didn't clean well, so it would be nice to have some replacements after the first one got dirty. Frank and Kyle rolled the hallway piece length-wise and walked it through the kitchen, past the cabinet hangers and the tile-layer, and then through the rear foyer and up the stairs. There was an inside corner that needed to be hand-stitched. Frank sat on the floor, legs splayed, middle finger thimble-capped, and began sewing the corner with wax nylon thread and a 4-inch needle. Kyle settled into his marginal linger, checking his phone and snapping his rubber bands.

"Why don't you go out and see if your uncle needs a hand with those throws," Frank said.

At the bottom of the stairs, Kyle flicked the finial just as Bruce Patton had, and it made that same dead sound. Any other day—any other house—Frank would have told him to keep his hands to himself. He would have gotten a mean joy out of disciplining the kid, setting him straight, but that impulse wasn't there. It came as a shock to Frank that he wouldn't have been angry had Kyle knocked the finial straight off the newel post. He suddenly envied the kid: the stupid ecstasy in which he moved, the casual disregard of everything around him. Frank had learned from his uncle to treat the customer's home as you would your own, but he decided that it wasn't a violation, it wasn't a betrayal of John to want to see that glass ball smashed, to identify—if only for a moment—with someone who just doesn't give a shit.

Frank pierced the sisal's latex backing and the needle surfaced between a row of cordage centimeters from the binding's inner edge. He drew out the thread, long and smooth and sure, and just caught a nip of the binding as he sent the needle back through and completed the stitch. This he could do for hours and never tire of its repetition. Yes, his fingertips would throb and his back would stiffen, but he suffered these in patience. He had never tried to put it into words, but he had always felt like sewing connected him to the past. Some of his tools were modern (the binder, the seamer), and some of them were more primitive (the tuck knife, the chisel). Needle and thread— they were like implements out of time, and whenever he took them up the same scene would play in his head as he was working: he was seated in a large tent with scores of other men, some older, some younger, and at the front of the tent was a horizontal loom from which a massive prayer rug was being steadily woven It had deep green flowers set against a field of dark blue, accented by figures of hanging lamps and ornate candlesticks. Its wool came from sheep that had grazed the mountains of Iran, and its dyes were born of those same highlands: blue from the indigo plant, red from the madder root, orange from the henna leaf, and brown from the gall nut. The tent was hot and Frank and the rest of the men were bare-chested, their skin slick with sweat. It was his job to sew into the corner of the rug the names of the men who had sacrificed their labor to bring it into being. One of the habits of the oriental rug maker was to autograph his creation, and for as many years as Frank had been entertaining this fiction, he had been stitching that long list of names of which his would be the last.

Rachel and Miranda came through the front door and P.J. bolted out to greet them. Rachel scooped him into her arms and the sisters climbed the stairs together, whispering to each other about the sisal.

"It smells like hay," Rachel said.

"Like the zoo," corroborated her older sister.

Miranda smiled at Frank and said hello as she walked past him with her violin case. Rachel hurried into the master bedroom and shut the door behind her. Frank heard P.J. bark once and Rachel telling him to keep quiet. It sounded as if she were up to no good, and Frank thought that maybe he should ask her to take the dog out of her mother's room, but then he knew that his jurisdiction here was limited. He might be accused of overstepping, or of trying to separate Rachel from the dog, who was her hero. Let *them* deal with it, he decided. This house needs fewer police, not more.

"I love it. I love the contrast between the dark binding and the stairs. I'm so glad that we painted them white."

"I love it too. Do you think we should put it on the back stairs when they're done?"

It was Connie and Elaine, standing in the foyer's medium light. Elaine had her arm around Connie, to brace her.

"That might be overkill," she said. "We don't want to make the same statement twice."

"No, you're right." Connie paused. "What about the finial?"

"What about it? It looks great."

"I like the glass and the hardware, but I don't know if it goes."

"The foyer didn't have a center. Remember? The finial gives it one. It's absolutely divine."

"I know. I'm being silly."

"It's a great little piece, a great little size. I love it."

"I love it too."

Elaine squeezed Connie's shoulder, and the two women leaned into each other until their temples touched and the one was no longer bracing the other. There had not been a moment like this between them in a long time. So many of their decisions had been reversed. They were surrounded by second, third, and fourth choices—in paint, wallpaper, molding, tile. But in Frank's stair runner there was a definitiveness, excusing it forever from doubt. It was wabi, more wabi than they had anticipated, and the success of their vision stunned them. The tenderness passing between the two women was as simple and as beautiful and as appropriate as the thing they were looking upon. How rare this had become.

Frank walked down two steps to the landing, distributing much of his weight to his left leg, which he now considered his "good" leg. It took a moment for the sight of Connie and Elaine to register with Frank. The fastidious glare was missing from Connie's eyes, and Elaine appeared almost sisterly. He didn't know what to make of them.

"Sorry I missed your calls," he said. "I don't always remember to carry my phone."

"When are you going to upgrade?" Elaine asked.

"Same day I get a website."

"The stairs look wonderful," Connie said.

"Thank you," said Frank, surprised at the lack of hesitation in his voice. He looked down and saw that he wasn't wearing any booties, but he didn't panic. He somehow knew that he wouldn't be harassed for it. He felt welcome in the eyes of these women, accepted, appreciated. Yesterday this would've been impossible. Maybe, because of his triumph on the stairs, he had acquitted himself, earned a kind of reprieve. He never saw the plumber wearing booties. Perhaps he, too, had reached this level of exception, if in fact it was real.

Rachel wobbled out of the master bedroom in a pair of her mother's black Ferragamo heels. Her fat little feet were far too small for the shoes, yet she managed to make it to the top of the stairs, her every step a gamble.

"Mom, look," she said, and bravely lowered herself onto the landing. "Mom," she said again, and Frank could tell that she wasn't doing this for fun. The set of her mouth, the daring in her steps—this was serious, purposeful, academic. She held onto the banister and stood upright, and from the other end of the house, battling through the din of constant, pervasive work, Miranda could be heard practicing scales on her violin.

"Mom, *look* at me!"

But Connie was talking to Elaine. She was looking at Rachel, but she couldn't see her. Her daughter desperately wanted her to see her. She was so proud that she had made it that far in the Ferragamos without falling. Frank saw the gap between her feet and the shoes, and how the strap, pulled to its last hole, failed her ankle, and his heart dropped in his chest. Keeping his voice low, he said, "I don't think your mom wants you walking on the new carpet in those shoes."

"What?" said Rachel, and as she turned around, she lost her balance and almost fell.

That's when Connie saw her, and all the hardness came back into her face, aging her ten years. "Where is the dog, Rachel?"

"I put him on your bed."

"Fuck," said Connie, her head giving an ugly jerk, as if the word had been shaken out of her. "He's not supposed to be in there. You *know* that."

She gained the second floor in a sustained spasm. She yelled the dog's name and scoured the bedroom carpet for skid marks while Frank stood in the doorway. She was in the sitting area, looking behind the chaise lounge, when P.J. came out of the closet and indicated with a plopping of his rump that he was about to scoot. Neither Frank nor

Connie reacted to his tinkling silver tags. In fact, they both froze—Connie out of hopelessness, an admission, really, that she would never reach the dog in time, and Frank out of a sheer sense of theater. The playhouse custodian is lying if he says he doesn't enjoy the show. The stage was set for the Modern Dog to befoul his master's chambers, and though it would be his job to scrub the smear after the lights came up, Frank was rapt.

P.J. seemed to sense that his will to scoot was stronger than the will of the humans in the room to stop it from happening. His round, black, pitiable eyes told a story of pain, a fire below, and of how this act, this self-squelching, would relieve it. There was nothing wretched in it, as attested to by Miranda's violin, which had not ceased playing, and would not until those sacs had been emptied and the dog liberated. He dug his forepaws into the carpet and his head floated back; his ears swung slightly and his eyelids fluttered. *Freedom on the other side, cool, cool release.* And already the paste was leaving his body, the hot mud pumping forth, but something was wrong. He was not going forward, he was going upward into someone's arms, and he could not rub the paste with his bottom, as he loved to do, because a hand was cupped there to collect it, a gentle yet confident hand that did not care whether it got dirty, a hand that he knew.

"I've had my eye on him since he came in here," said Gildea. "Not to worry."

More veterinarian than housekeeper, she spirited P.J. into the bathroom and Connie raced to the spot where he'd been sitting. There were no traces; Gildea had caught it all. Connie looked up at the coffered ceiling. "Oh, thank God," she sighed. Then she looked at Frank, and the relief in her eyes vanished, and for a moment Frank thought that she was angry with him, that somehow *he* was responsible for the dog's behavior. She flew into the bathroom and Frank heard her ridiculing P.J. and—despite Gildea's protests—landing him a swat.

"Now that's something he can't help," said Gildea, weighing her words. "He just wants to be rid of the stuff. It burns him up inside. How's he to know he's doing it on the new carpet?"

"He can't walk up three steps for the trainer," Connie said, "but he can drag his dirty little ass all over the house. If *that* was part of the test, I wouldn't be bringing him back on Friday for a re-take."

Elaine came in with the Ferragamos and returned them to their proper place in the menagerie. She crossed into the bathroom and closed the door behind her, as much to imprison the dog as to muffle Connie's tirade. Miranda had stopped practicing, and Frank took this as a reminder: there is a job waiting for you, there is work yet to be done. He went into the hallway and picked up the needle, thimble, and spool of wax thread. Rachel was sitting on the floor, rubbing her toes. Halfway down the stairs, Frank glanced back at her, and though her eyes refused to answer his, he could see that she had been crying.

CHAPTER SEVEN

That evening, Frank drove to the office of the chiropractor, Dr. Temoyan. It was in a small complex of three-story brick buildings just off West Chester Pike, not two miles from his house. During the ride over, a thunderstorm burst upon the world, scattering flashes of white-green light across the sky. Frank pulled into the parking lot just as the rains were tapering off. Thankful for the delay, he sat in his car and watched yellow steam rising from the cooled blacktop. Its movement away from the office touched off a jealousy in Frank, a vague desire to be something other than solid. He did not go in until the last of the vapor had lifted.

"Frank Renzetti," he told the secretary. "My wife made the appointment."

He filled out some forms, and after two pages of a *Field & Stream* article, the doctor called him back. Temoyan was olive-skinned and pudgy with coarse black hair, silver-framed glasses, and a goatee of such precision that Frank thought it had been drawn on with a Sharpie. He wore the clean white overcoat of all doctors, and this detail made

Frank less suspicious of him. Temoyan had him lay back on the paper-stripped examining table.

"How long have you had this pain?" he asked.

"About a month," said Frank, "but it only really started hurting me last Friday."

"And is the pain constant, or does it come and go?"

"It's pretty much always there. The only time I don't feel it is in the morning when I wake up."

"And the pain starts while you're still in bed, or when you go to stand up?"

"When I bend over the sink to splash water in my face. The muscle gets real tight and it feels like I pulled something."

Temoyan lifted Frank's right leg and slowly raised it, stopping when it was perpendicular to his torso.

"How is the pain now?" he asked.

"The same," Frank said. "Just kind of a gnawing in that one spot."

"Turn over onto your stomach."

Frank changed positions, doing his best not to rip the paper, as Temoyan pulled a Thumper from a shelf along the wall. The Thumper had a short, gray handle and a black, diamond-shaped head with four rotating balls at its points and one at its center. Frank knew it from a late-night TV commercial, but had never expected to actually see it in someone's possession. He didn't believe that products like the Thumper had a life beyond the screen; he thought they were all scams and gimmicks. Temoyan switched on the Thumper and Frank almost laughed when the balls started buzzing and vibrating.

"I don't think you have sciatica," Temoyan said.

"No?"

"No. It's your hamstring."

He rested the Thumper on the back of Frank's thigh and began riding it over the muscles. "How's that for you?" he asked.

"Fine," said Frank. His sly, one-sided grin had evened itself out into a lazy rictus, giving him a drugged look. "It feels like the massage chair at the mall."

Temoyan chuckled. "That was some storm," he said. "We lost power for a minute."

"It was pretty bad," said Frank, his voice shaking along with the machine.

"Just let me know if it starts to hurt."

"Sure thing."

Temoyan tightened his grip on the handle and steered the Thumper in a controlled spiral, turning it slightly as he went. He was commanding the instrument now, not just allowing it to run. He made several passes this way, and on the last one he dug the machine deep into the muscle. He heard no objection from Frank, but when he lifted the Thumper to knead a different section, Frank's mesh shorts came with it. The fabric was caught in the center ball, drawn up in a little cyclone. Temoyan kept his cool, thinking that if he continued the massage, the greedy ball would eventually give up the shorts. It did not, and the longer the Thumper ran the more fabric the ball gathered, tugging enough away to reveal Frank's boxers. Temoyan shut off the machine and quickly went to work on the snag.

Frank lay with his eyes closed and his mouth still agape. His slackened arms hung on either side of the table like static pendulums, his index fingers just touching the floor. He could sense that the joyous quaking had stopped, but was not yet aware that his underwear was showing. In the

Thumper's immediate afterglow, he felt like a piece of ten-derized meat, the taut and tough gone out of him. The pain in his leg was no longer there, replaced by a savory numb-ness. He opened his eyes and saw the mold of a crooked human spine in the corner of the room, and was grateful it was not his.

"Helen!" Dr. Temoyan called. "Can you come in here with a pair of scissors, please?"

"What do you need scissors for?" asked Frank.

Temoyan hesitated, then: "Your shorts are caught and I can't get them out."

Frank propped himself up on his elbows and looked over his shoulder. "Damn thing felt so good, I didn't even notice."

"The Thumper is very effective," said Temoyan, taking the scissors from Helen and studiously cutting away the fabric.

The visit cost Frank thirty dollars—and a cookie-sized hole in the seat of his Champions. He scheduled another appointment for the following Tuesday and strolled out to his car. Crossing the parking lot, he felt as light and as free as that scrolling yellow vapor, but as he was sitting behind the wheel, running the wipers to clear what was left of the rainwater, the pain came back. Not all at once, but grad-ually, like a child waking from a nap. Frank shifted his weight to his left buttocks, held the position and waited for a change. Nothing. He got out and stood by the car, staring at the traffic on West Chester Pike, tensing his hamstring and then relaxing it. He did this a half-dozen times. Still nothing. He listened to the wipers screeching against the dry windshield, and reached into his pocket for the disc of red fabric Temoyan had made him keep as a souvenir of the mishap. He held it in his hand, squeezed it, thought about tossing it away, then, with a violent snap of his arm, shoved it into his mouth.

He chewed on it the whole way home.

FRANK TURNED OFF the baseball game at ten o'clock and went upstairs to get ready for bed. He scrubbed his teeth, gurgled with mouthwash, and popped three Advil to quiet his leg. He hit the bathroom light and stood for a moment in the darkened hallway. Above the murmur of Donna's true crime show he heard a loud sucking noise. Walking into the bedroom, he tried not to look at the source, but as it tends to be with the perverse, spectacle is stronger than protest. He glanced to his left and saw Donna in bed with the covers pulled down and Ferdinand splayed across her chest. The cat's mouth was adhered to a spot on her neck, and he was working it over like a ravenous cub latched at his mother's teat.

"Is he ever going to grow out of that?" Frank asked with a sneer.

"Grow out of suckies?" said Donna in a childish voice. "Never."

"As many times as I've seen him do it, it still makes me uncomfortable."

Frank twisted off his wedding band and threw it carelessly onto the dresser. Ferdinand stopped slurping and turned his massive orange head to look at Frank. Seeing nothing of consequence in the man, he greedily resumed the hickey.

"He was taken away from his mother too soon," Donna explained, stroking Ferdinand's haunches. "He was never properly weaned."

"You've been telling me that for twelve years. At what point does it become bestiality?"

"At no point," laughed Donna.

Frank sat on the edge of the bed and rubbed anti-fungal cream between his toes. "You both get off on it," he grumbled.

"I do *not* get off on it. I let him do suckies because I know it makes him feel good. It calms him down."

"Calms him down from what? He does nothing all day, and then he rests afterward. If anybody should be sucking, it's me."

"Why? Because of your leg?"

"It has nothing to do with that."

"Please. You've been miserable since you got home from the doctor's."

"I'd hesitate to call him a doctor."

Donna sighed heavily, and Ferdinand paused to ride the swell of her chest. "It doesn't always take the first time, Frank. You have to go more than once. Give the guy a chance before you write him off completely."

As if to emphasize this, Ferdinand started in again, smacking with such brio that Frank grabbed his pillow and stamped over to Paul's room.

A few moments later, Donna called out across the hall, "He's gone. You scared him away."

"I'm sorry," said Frank.

"It's okay. He was done anyway."

This was neither an invitation for Frank to join her in the bed nor a pardon of his sulkiness. He had created a distance between them, and his punishment was to keep it, at least until morning. His tone would be softer then. He and Donna would eat breakfast together, and there would be no talk of the cat or the chiropractor; they would discuss the trip to Ventnor, which was only three days away. In fact, Paul had called Donna that afternoon and asked her to bring down his swim fins. The idea of removing something—*anything*—from Paul's room to make way for the renovation appealed to the worker in Frank, that most constant part of him. Because he knew that he would forget to in the morning, he clicked on the bedside lamp, shuffled over to the closet, and lifted the heavy black flippers from a hook on the door. He turned them upside-down and dry sand sprinkled onto the carpet. Frank swept his foot across the grains and a few of them stuck to his toes. It was an odd sensation, but he rather liked it: a landlocked approximation of the beach. He leaned the fins against the nightstand and climbed back into his son's bed, thinking about the night when Paul, just turned fourteen, had accompanied him to Melboldt for a measurement.

Melboldt was a large communal campus in the woodlands of Montgomery County for people living with developmental disabilities. The residents stayed in ranch-style houses, each one with its own name. Frank had been called out to measure the common room in Marissa House, and because the room was so spacious, 15' × 50', he needed Paul to hold the other end of the tape measure for him so he could get an accurate read. According to the house manager, one of the residents was obsessively pulling yarn from the carpet seams, leaving frayed gaps in the middle of the high traffic area. People were tripping over the gaps and wheelchairs were getting stuck in them. The rug needed to be replaced before someone got hurt. This gave the measurement an unlikely urgency, another reason why Frank wanted Paul to come along. He thought the humanitarian drama might turn him on to carpet work, which, at that point in Paul's life, existed as a mere abstraction, not a livelihood or a career, just a thing his father did to make money.

When Frank and Paul arrived at Marissa House, the residents, most of whom had Downs Syndrome, were gathered in the common room. A few were sitting at a table in the far corner, playing UNO with the house manager. A heavyset girl in a striped sweater was standing before a dry erase board, drawing line after line of miniature tornadoes with a squeaky black marker. The TV was on but no one was watching it, perhaps because a boy had parked his wheelchair directly in front of the screen, and was blasting Michael Jackson's "Human Nature" from a boom box in his lap. A short black girl with colorful beads in her hair roamed the floor, stopping here and there to dance to the music. Her right hand was limp and deformed, and flapped amphibiously on her delicate wrist. She seemed the most energized by Marissa's guests, and took to following them around.

This made Paul uncomfortable, and seeing what was happening, the house manager scolded the girl, whose name was Genesis. "Genesis," said the house manager, a quick-tongued Trinidadian woman, "you leave them two alone. They wouldn't be here if not for you." But Genesis kept on hounding them, interfering with their work by standing on the tape measure so they couldn't rewind it. "What did I *say*?" the house manager shouted, and took Genesis by the shoulders and directed her to the UNO table.

She remained in her seat, but she couldn't take her eyes off Paul: she was smitten with him. The last measure-

ment required him to get close to Genesis, and as he knelt
beside her she leaned over and kissed him on the mouth.
"I love you," she said. "I love you. I love you. I love you."
Paul scampered back a few feet and looked hard at Frank,
embarrassment reddening his face and neck.

Anticipating further amours, the boy with the radio
started wheeling himself closer to the UNO table. Before
he could run over the tape measure, Frank flipped the lock
to reel it back in, and Paul's end jumped out of his hand,
slicing the tip of his index finger and drawing blood. He
shot up and cursed under his breath. Genesis saw that he
was bleeding and went over and hugged him, cuffing her
arms around his waist and butting her head against his
chest, those multi-colored beads swaying and clacking.

The house manager came around the table and yanked
Genesis away. "But I love him!" Genesis protested. "I love
him! I do!" She reached out and affectionately stroked
Paul's bleeding finger.

That sent the house manager over the edge.

"What are you doing, huh? Who do you think you are?"
and she grabbed Genesis by the wrist and smacked her
demi-hand. "What you gon' do—marry him!?"

Genesis started bawling. The boy in the wheelchair,
stalled in one of the carpet gaps, laughed and beat the top
of his radio, while the girl at the dry erase board stoically
put down her marker and escorted Genesis and the house
manager out of the common room.

Five years passed before Frank asked for his son's help
again. It was Paul's freshman year at Drexel University,
and he was home for spring break. Frank had a mammoth
installation at a car dealership in South Philly, almost 300
yards of carpet, and he was a man short. They weren't

allowed to start working until after the dealership closed for the day and everybody went home, which meant that the job stretched well into the following morning; it was 3 a.m. by the time they finally got back to the warehouse. Frank worked Paul to exhaustion that night, and he ached for days afterward, vexed by the stubborn soreness in his hands and feet. Frank said that the pain was a memory of the good work he'd done, and that he should honor it rather than fight it. "Where the hell did you get that from?" Paul had asked. It was something Frank's uncle had preached, and long ago he had taken it to heart, but lately, with his leg recalling little but the house on Dunwoody Lane, he had begun to question the old adage.

Maybe pain *is* bullshit, he thought. Maybe Paul's right and Ace is wrong. Maybe I need to get out before Genesis makes those gaps any bigger and I fall the hell in. I never told Paul what the house manager said to me on the phone the next day. She said they found the yarn from the carpet hidden under Genesis's bed, but they didn't find all of it. She said Genesis liked to eat things she shouldn't: stickers, shampoo. I bet when she leaned in to kiss him, Paul smelled it on her breath—the dirty old rug. And I bet he smells it every time he looks at me. And how could he not? It's in me like it was in her, except I can't hide the fact. It's my very life.

CHAPTER EIGHT

After Frank had seen Rachel crying on Tuesday afternoon, he had gone out to the garage to collect the sisal throw rugs that he had asked Billy to bind. Billy and Kyle were kneeling on the concrete floor, and Billy had the binder slanted back and was peering into the undercarriage. Like evidence, a partially bound throw rug sat next to Kyle, its face littered with an unusual amount of castoff thread. Kyle looked at the rug but not at Frank, sagging his head and letting his bangs fall in a veil over his eyes.

"What happened?" Frank asked.

Billy eased the binder forward onto its wheels and cleaned some grease off his hands with the front of his shirt. He was sweating badly.

"I let Kyle run the binder," he said, "just to give him a taste. He was going good, but then it jammed up on him." He turned to Kyle, the empathetic uncle. "You were pulling the machine faster than you could feed the carpet in, right?"

Kyle nodded, but still he kept his head down.

"What made you think Percman could run the binder?" Frank asked.

"He told me he was tired of watching," shrugged Billy. "I was right there with him the whole time. He just got nervous."

They futzed around with the binder for about thirty minutes, and determined that the timing gauge was damaged, and therefore needed to be replaced. Frank took the binder home with him and early Wednesday morning drove up to Northwest Philly to see Gord the repairman at HPK, the shop where Frank had bought the binder in 1997.

When Frank got there, Gord was sitting at a long wooden table in a workroom at the back of the shop. He wore dark blue jeans and an unbuttoned green polo, its faded collar upturned at the tips. He had a broad boxer's nose, cheeks portioned out in lumps, and a forehead of tiered wrinkles. Around the sides of his head wound a fluffy ring of silver hair, complemented by a pair of identical silver rope chains that hung just above his clavicle. Frank liked Gord, liked him a great deal, and he liked his workroom, too, with its white pegboard of tools, its orphaned parts strewn about the table, its metal stool and flattened seat cushion, its screwdrivers of all lengths and sizes in their plastic yellow bin, its skeins of yarn and binding, and its permanent odor of degreaser, the spray lube that Frank always found to have a tropical note to it, coconut or macadamia—he couldn't quite place it. Though it was mechanical failure that periodically brought Frank to Gord's lair, the visits themselves were a balm to man as well as machine. It was a place of honest work and honest talk, and he believed there were very few like it left in the world.

Gord put aside what he had been working on and started dismantling the binder's timing gauge.

"I took it out yesterday and put it back in," Frank said, "but I couldn't get it to go."

"Your screws are shot," said Gord, "and the lower shaft bevel gear is all torqued. I'll have to get you a new one of those, too."

"You have one on hand?"

"I have a little bit of everything on hand."

Gord loosened the timing screws and jimmied out the lower shaft, then blew dust from the undercarriage with a can of compressed air.

"You been busy?" Frank asked.

"Fits and starts. You know how it is."

"That guy from New York still coming in?"

"Yeah. He was here last week. Trigger switch went on him."

"I still can't believe there's nobody up there who services these machines."

"There aren't many people who even *use* these machines. Your casual customer isn't interested, and most contractors are afraid of 'em, or they're too impatient to learn."

Gord had retrieved the new shaft and timing gauge from a supply closet and was opening their boxes and placing the parts in neat little piles on the table. An oscillating fan mounted on the wall blew both sets of instructions to the floor. Frank picked them up.

"You need these?" he asked.

Gord shook his head and Frank tossed the booklets into a trashcan under the table. An empty bottle of fish oil pills stood out from the rest of the waste.

"Does it work?" Frank asked.

"What?"

"The fish oil."

"I don't know. I've only been taking it for a month. My neighbor swears by it."

"My wife keeps telling me to take it. Although I don't know if I should listen to her medical advice anymore."

"Why not?"

"She sent me to her chiropractor."

"What for?"

"My leg."

"What'd the guy do—feel you up?"

"He pulled my shorts down, but not intentionally."

"Sounds about right," Gord said. "They're all perverts, but they don't mean to be." He was tightening the screws on the bevel gear with a tiny, black-handled screwdriver. "What's wrong with your leg?"

"The guy says it's a pulled hamstring. He used a Thumper on me."

"That thing from TV?"

"Yeah. It almost put me to sleep. It felt great at the time, but then it wore off. The pain came back."

"Thousand bucks it's sciatica."

"He said it wasn't."

"That's because he wants to keep Thumpin' you. The problem's not your leg; it's your back. All that lifting you do, you probably slipped a disk."

"But my back doesn't hurt."

"It doesn't have to, not when you got all those nerves and shit in there."

Gord sprayed the new parts with degreaser and clamped shut the housing for the timing gear. He took a spool of binding from the pegboard and fed it through the guides, and after pausing to adjust the drape of his necklaces, fished a carpet scrap out of the trash and cut it into a rect-

angle with a large pair of shears. With the fan on its back-
swing, fluttering the hair above his right ear, Gord fit the
scrap beneath the needle, pulled the trigger switch, and
applied the tape as easily as if it were the machine's grand
unveiling.

"You're back in business," he said. "Now just keep it
away from your third in command and you should be
fine."

FRANK ARRIVED at the warehouse shortly after nine
and saw that Billy's car wasn't parked out front. Towing
Kyle around sometimes made him late, but never this late.
Frank went inside and called Billy's phone, left a quick,
nasty message on his voicemail. Then he called Billy's girlfriend, Christy, and she picked up after one ring, her voice
scratchy and weak. It sounded like the previous night had
not been good to her, so Frank, who had always thought
of Christy as a saint for putting up with Billy, lightened
his tone.

"Hey, Christy."

"Hey, Frank."

"You have any idea where Billy and Kyle are?"

Stiffly, as if she were holding back tears, Christy said,
"They're in Lima Correctional."

"Lima Correctional? For what?"

"Upper Darby did a big drug bust last night, and Billy
and Kyle got taken in with a bunch of other people. I told
Billy I didn't want Kyle coming to stay with us. I knew
this was going to happen."

"Did they set bail yet?"

"That's what I'm trying to find out. I'm actually sitting
here with my dad's lawyer."

Frank thought of Billy's ten-year-old daughter. "Does Vanessa know?" he asked.

"No. Thank God they picked them up at the bar and not here. I just dropped her off at her friend's. I don't know how I'm going to tell her."

"Have you talked to Billy?"

"He called me this morning. You know him: he thinks the whole thing's a joke. He thinks he's getting out today. It's a lot more serious than that. He said his dad would help him with bail, but he's all the way out in California, and I'm having a hard time getting a hold of him." Christy paused, gathering herself with a sniffle, a swallow. "What are you gonna do without him? Billy said you guys were working on a big job. He would have to go and pull this shit now."

"Don't worry about me," said Frank. "I'll worry about me. Just take care of Vanessa and call me when you hear something."

Egging him on a little, Christy said, "It's okay, Frank."

"What do you mean it's okay?"

"It's okay if you want to call him a fuckin' idiot?"

"You're giving me permission?"

"I am. Not like you need it."

"Okay," relished Frank, "he's a *fuckin'* idiot, and his nephew's worth about as much as a pimple on a rat's ass."

Christy laughed, and Frank laughed with her, and before solemnity could return, they said their goodbyes and hung up. Frank looked at the clock on his desk: half past nine. Connie and Company were no doubt wondering where he was. He called Elaine and told her that he was running late. She said she understood, but there was restlessness in her voice, the passing of yesterday's hard-earned respect. Frank decided then and there to keep this new calamity a secret. He would say that Billy and Kyle were out on another job, a lie of temporary convenience, and, to take up the slack, he would do as much of the day's work as he could by himself. He sighed at the thought of it, but refused to lament the delinquency of fate.

To punish him for breaking the binder, Frank had made Kyle load the rug and pad for today. Three second-floor bedrooms and a loft were on the schedule. The carpet for these spaces was called Beachfront Vista, a high-end cut pile in saffron and cream from a boutique mill in Georgia. Turning out of the warehouse driveway, Frank rested his right hand on the topmost roll of carpet. It felt solid beneath his palm, like ballast. Cut-pile was among the easiest goods to work with, and because the bedrooms and the loft were each less than twelve feet wide, he wouldn't have to seam on any fill pieces. He had that much going for him.

Frank noticed two things about the Silberstein house as he was walking toward the garage. The first was the landscaper. Just as on Friday, he was petting the burl on the old silver maple. The Amish were coming that morning to excise the nodule, and in this their final intimacy, the landscaper touched his forehead to the burl's knaggy cheek and wrapped his arms around it as far as he could stretch them. The second thing Frank noticed was all the open windows on the first and second floor, from whose dark cavities men's voices howled, revolting against the heat and the Democratic party. Frank saw the plumber—who also serviced the house's HVAC system—leaning against the dumpster and pressing a cold bottle of water to the back of his neck.

"Just a word of warning to you," he said to Frank. "The

air conditioning's gonna be out until at least noon. The fan died on the big unit. I got a guy driving out the part from Jersey. He's usually pretty fast, but I'm not his only stop."

He opened the water and gulped down half the bottle. There seemed to be few spots on his clean-shaven head that weren't bubbling with sweat. He took out his handkerchief and gave his crown a universal swipe.

"Where'd you get the water?" Frank asked.

"The fridge in the garage," Bruce said. He poured some into his hand and splashed it on his face. "Don't tell anybody."

Frank set down the binder in the corner of the garage and went over to the refrigerator. Someone had taken the A and the N from Kyle's "PERCMAN" and spelled out a new message with the alphabet magnets: DOGZ ANUS. Frank opened the door, thinking, I'm not going to take one. I just want to see how many are in here, for later. He stood in the polar breath of the humming appliance, taking stock of its bounty of drinks: water, Gatorade, juice boxes, wine cooler. There was even a bottle of champagne.

"Easy there, big fella. Those are for paying customers only."

Frank shut the refrigerator and turned to see Vic entering the garage through the family entry door, his protuberant gut vainly corseted by a half-tucked-in golf shirt. He plodded over the bound sisal throw rugs as if they weren't even there.

"Watch those," said Frank.

Vic looked at the refrigerator door. "Who keeps fuckin' with these magnets?" he groaned, pushing the letters into a cluster at the bottom of the door. "Did one of your guys do that?"

"My guys aren't even here," Frank replied.

"What happened? They call out sick? Too much Southern Comfort last night?"

Bruce came out from behind the dumpster and sought the shade of the garage. He had smartly finished his water and disposed of it in private.

"They're picking up some Orientals in Flourtown," said Frank, testing out his story.

"Orientals? I thought you just did rugs. I didn't know you were into human trafficking." Vic laughed and his heavy, bouncing shoulders caused a lock of slicked-back hair to fall out of place and divide his cliff-like forehead. "How do you think he does it?" Vic asked Bruce. "I bet he stuffs 'em inside the rugs like shrimps in an egg roll. He probably does the same thing with the Mexicans, but he makes burritos out of them. You like burritos, Bruce?"

Reluctantly playing along, Bruce said, "I don't know if I'd want to eat that kind of burrito."

"If it had one of them nice mamasitas in there you would. You'd take a big bite out of that *culo grande*, wouldn't you?"

A new generation of sweat had begun to form on Bruce's scalp. Vic sidled up to him and slapped him on the back. Amid the ribbing and razzing that followed, Vic said to Frank, "One mamasita burrita for Bruce. The sooner you get it for him, the sooner he fixes the air. Eh?"

"Today's not the day to be busting my stones," said Frank.

"Oh, no? What's so special about today? You announcing your retirement?"

"No, but you'd probably like that."

"Sure, but then I'd have to get another carpet guy to replace you, and there's a good chance I wouldn't like him either."

"And why's that?"

"Because you're all low-lifes." These words of Vic's were sharper than before, steelier. "Every carpet guy I've ever known has been a low-life."

Frank stood directly in front of Vic, who was taller than him by a good six inches. The man loomed, consigning Frank—and everything around him—to shadow. Frank was intimidated, but he wouldn't give Vic the pleasure of seeing that he was. He stared up into his crow-black eyes and, without flinching, asked, "Do I look like a low-life to you?"

"You're a little more polished than most," said Vic, "but those two guys you got with you—they're a couple of dirt merchants."

"I'm not talking about them. I'm talking about me. What makes you think *I'm* a low-life?"

"You spend your whole life working on the ground, don't you?" His brow vaulted in mock epiphany. "There you go: Low . . . life."

Doing his best Mills Lane, the plumber stepped between the two men, keeping them from getting any closer. Vic moved back, still with that look of ironic illumination. Frank burned to punch him, maybe would have had it not been for Bruce. More than that, he wanted to slice open his belly with a carpet knife, something he had never wished upon anyone before. The knife was right there on the ground next to the binder. All he had to do was pick it up and swing—he was bound to hit that gut. It took a true invention of will, a beating back of coarser blood, but Frank stayed his itching hand.

Vic walked over to the port-a-potty and gave it a stiff shove. "Guess what, fellas? We're gettin' a new Mexican space shuttle today." Recovering some of his earlier frivolity, he pointed at Frank. "You better make sure you use it. Wouldn't want those cockroach test pilots to die in vain."

Frank sat down in the corner of the garage with the binder between his legs and started working on Kyle's abandoned throw rug. He couldn't focus very well; the altercation with Vic had left him jangled. For years he had suffered the prejudices of customers and contractors, and on all of those occasions he had kept his mouth shut, he had resisted the urge to defend his profession, choosing instead to ignore the insults, even when they had cut deep. He never fought back because he shared their criticism, he agreed with their low opinion of the industry. It was overrun with hacks and butchers and fly-by-nighters, unschooled and unskilled. His very own Carpet Ape was an imaginary reaction to this state of affairs, his personal indictment of all that was wrong with the trade. But he had vowed long ago to not become the thing they so maligned. He would evolve along with the work, he would be better and do better, he would stand apart from the savagery of his cohorts. And he had achieved this, even if Billy and Kyle had not. He had made himself an artisan in a field where there were none, and this he could vouch for, and vouch for it he did in the face of that *cafone*. Yet even with the satisfaction of having finally opened his mouth, Frank knew that his pride had been futile, that in the eyes of the world he was still just a paid groveler, and this brought him shame—for himself, for Billy and Kyle, and yes, even for the Carpet Ape, his notorious brother-in-arms.

Since it had the least amount of furniture, Frank thought he would attack the loft first. As he was passing through the kitchen with a toolbox, he saw Connie and Elaine in the planning center. Elaine was showing Connie different swatches of fabric pinned to a poster board. Frank waved at Elaine and she tossed him a quick, businesslike smile. Connie, seated amid her gallery of hand-drawn graph paper, was so engrossed in the look and feel of the swatches that she never saw Frank walk by. He welcomed this lack of attention. Though he had already lied to Vic, he was no less nervous about deceiving the ladies, Connie in particular. Those inky lashes could be used to beat the truth right out of him. Unless interrogated, silence would be his default setting for the rest of the day, that and scarcity.

At the foot of the stairs leading up to the loft, he found P.J. knocked out from the heat. It appeared as if he had been stationed there to guard the loft from trespassers but had succumbed to the extreme closeness of the air and was now lying on his side with his head rolled back, exposing a masculine V-neck of flocculent black hair that Frank had not seen in that spot before, and which made him laugh. Frank stirred him with his sneaker and the dog lazily got to his feet and let Frank through. P.J. watched him out of swollen, weeping eyes, and, echoing his surrogate father, Bruce Patton, yapped a single word of caution to the unlucky ascender.

The thermostat on the second floor read 90°. The temperature in the loft, the highest point in the house, was ten degrees hotter. It was like crossing over into something solid, a static mass that neither moved nor allowed movement. There were no windows in the long, narrow room, just a pair of sky lights that had been painted shut. The resulting air had form and weight, and as Frank breathed it in, he could feel himself getting denser, heavier.

The old rug and pad came out easy. He stacked them by the curb and brought up the new rolls of felt, making several trips to the van. He paused to check his phone on the dashboard, hoping for a call or a message from Christy, but there was nothing. He also stopped on the side of the garage to drink from a garden hose the contractors had turned into a private drinking fountain. After being given the okay by the stone mason, the fountain's lookout, Frank lapped at the cool, rust-tinged water, and let it course through his hair and down his back. The secret spring refreshed him—until, that is, he returned to the loft. As the sun neared its zenith, the room was room getting hotter.

In conditions like these, Uncle John would tell the story of the old Italian sulfur miners, invulnerable men who made their living deep in the bowels of the Cozzo Disi, their uniform a mere loincloth, and sometimes not even that. Like burrowing infants, they fled the light for twelve hours a day in that continental furnace, ingenious movers and shakers prevailing upon the rock with sledge and bucket, powered by a blood more animal than human. Frank thought of them now in his tunnel in the sky, and because every garment was a cage, and because he was alone, without anyone to make him feel self-conscious, he did as the miners, stripping down to his boxers and crawling to his work.

For a short while, the shedding of his clothes delivered Frank. He felt thinner, younger, faster, stronger. With that four-legged blood conducting his limbs, he stapled the first and second rolls of pad without needing a break, but by the third roll Frank began to list, his vision to blur. He looked up at the skylights and the sun screamed down at him from its tyrannical post. He dropped the stapler, and the sound it made when it hit the floor hardly traveled—like a clap underwater. He grew dizzy, his muscles tensed, sweat streamed from his head, his armpits, his crotch, though it was powerless to cool him. Through the confusion and fatigue, one thing was clear: he had to get out of that room or he was going to faint. He bunched up his clothes and staggered down the stairs.

To the men who saw him, he looked like a philanderer escaping his girlfriend's husband. One man, the carpenter, thought that Frank was getting ready to streak in protest of the house's Official Renovation Complex, at the head of which sat the triumvirate of Connie, Vic, and Elaine. Frank didn't care how these men perceived him, only that none of them be drinking from the hose when he got there. Except for the stone mason, Frank had the fountain to himself. He pitched his clothes into the grass and genuflected before the spout. He could not get enough of it.

"Watch you don't drown," cautioned the watchman.

Frank gasped and wiped the water from his eyes. He looked at the stone mason. He was a short, impish man in ripped denim shorts with a blue bandana tied loosely around his tanned neck. He stood in the shadow of the garage, mechanically flipping a trowel and catching it by the handle.

"I can't go back up there," Frank blurted. "Not until the air's fixed."

"No telling when that'll be," the stone mason said. "Crazy as it sounds, I'm almost thankful to be working outside today." He peeped around the corner of the garage. "I don't mind you drinking, but if Vic hears this running too long, it's my ass."

"Vic can go to hell," Frank said, "where I've been for the past hour."

"I'm just trying to keep everyone happy. You know how it is."

Frank thrust the hose down the front of his boxers and drenched his genitalia.

"Come on, man," the stone mason objected, fumbling his trowel. "You expect anyone to drink outta there after that?"

Frank closed his eyes and smiled broadly as the water gushed about his privates. He ran the hose until he was sure that he could move again in a world that was not tar. He lay in the grass to dry, a hunk of beached driftwood, convinced that what had just happened to him was heat stroke, the beginnings of it, anyway. Donna had warned him about it at breakfast, but he told her not to worry, the house was air-conditioned. He'd be working inside all day, except when it was time to get the rugs, and that never takes more than a couple of minutes. Donna said it doesn't matter. For a guy his age, two minutes of hard work in this kind of heat is the same as two hours. Frank considered taking back what he had said to Gord about no longer listening to his wife's medical advice. Her forebodings, paranoid as they sometimes were, came from a need to preserve him, to keep him whole and alive. Sooner or later he would have to accept her belief that any provocation to invincibility was just not worth the sulfur.

Pulling on his clothes, Frank became aware of something happening on the front lawn. He heard a pair of bickering voices, a burst of laughter and applause. He straightened his hair with his fingers and walked around to the front of the house, not entirely shocked by what he saw.

Beneath the silver maple a crowd of workers had gathered: the carpenter, the tile-layer, the painters, the electricians. Bruce Patton hung off to the left, and next to him stood a muscular Amish man with a broad-brimmed straw hat and a pointy blond beard. He held at the ready a six-foot crosscut saw, its other end supported by the woodworker's son, a fine-haired boy of twelve in black shoes and suspenders. The attention of all was turned to Vic and the landscaper, who, staged upon the tree's roots, were debating its future. It wouldn't have one, the landscaper was arguing, if the Amish were allowed to scavenge its burl.

"If they cut off this growth," he said, placing a protective hand on the burl, "the tree dies. It's that simple."

Vic was incredulous. "The tree's not gonna die," he said. "We'll throw some latex paint and some Listerine on there. It'll be fine."

"Latex and Listerine?" mocked the landscaper. "All that does is make the wound look better; it doesn't stop the tree from dying."

"And so what if it dies? We chop it down and we're done with it. That's a thousand less leaves you have to rake this fall."

The landscaper stepped closer to the maple, giving Vic a clearer view of Dunwoody Lane. "Look around at these other houses," he said. "Do you see any silver maples? Do you see *any* trees over fifteen feet? No, because they got rid of them all when they 'dozed this land for houses. All of them except one—this tree right here," and he stepped away from the trunk, balancing on the uneven roots. "It's an old tree," he continued. "It may only be around for another ten years, but the key to its future—the future of the silver maple in general, if you think about it—is locked up inside this bunion." He smiled, crazily, and tears shone in his lidless eyes, but the rigor of his conviction would not let them fall. "When the tree dies, the burl will kick out its clone, an identical twin that'll live another hundred years. You let these guys hack off the burl prematurely, the tree's legacy is over."

Vic cleared his throat of phlegm, startling the Amish boy, almost making him drop his end of the saw. "Can someone explain to me why we're even arguing over this thing," he said. "I mean, look at it."

Everyone took a long look at the burl.

"Reminds me of the Elephant Man," said Vic. "It's hideous."

"On the outside," said the Amish man. "On the inside the wood is quite beautiful, quite rare. It will make a table unlike most that you buy in stores, unusually pretty."

"A conversation piece," said the landscaper. "Something to talk about with guests."

Frank heard the front door open and slam shut. Then Connie was slashing through the mulch, parting the boxwoods with her sculpted calves. As she tore across the lawn, the workers shifted and murmured and glanced at each other nervously. The only two who weren't behaving like embarrassed schoolchildren were the Amish man and his son.

"Why is Mr. Stoltzfus just standing there?" Connie asked Vic. "Why is he not working?"

"Because Seeley thinks he's going to kill the tree," said Vic.

"Is that right, Mr. Stoltzfus?" Connie inquired of the Amish man. "Are you going to kill the tree?"

Mr. Stoltzfus straightened up in his broadfall trousers, and his son did the same.

"My business is with the burl," he said, "not the tree. Though it has been my experience that maples are very hard to kill, even a one as old as this. A single burl slab from its trunk won't harm it but a little."

"We're not talking about a 'slab,'" Seeley whined. "We're talking about *eternity.*"

High above in their hidden bleachers, the cicadas, which had been cycling without cease, curtailed their strident vibrato and suddenly went silent. Frank couldn't be sure that it wasn't a trick of the heat, but he thought he saw Connie's dark eyelashes lengthening. In that brief moment before the cicadas started up again, Frank looked at Seeley, so loyal a guardian, and felt deeply for the short, smut-faced man, as did all the workers. They knew that Seeley was about to be scourged—how it *hurt* to watch the holy fool come out of him—and they doubted whether he or his burl would survive it.

"I've been listening to your bullshit about this tree for the past two months," Connie said. "It didn't make any sense to me the first time, and it doesn't make any sense to me now. What makes you think I'm going to believe you over him?"

"Because I know what I'm talking about," Seeley said. He indicated Mr. Stoltzfus with a backward jerk of his thumb. "Just because he's Amish doesn't mean he knows what's best for the tree. He could be a poacher for all we know."

Vic and Connie both laughed, and even Mr. Stoltzfus couldn't hide a smile.

"It's not funny. Burl poaching in the Redwoods is an environmental crime, with fines up to $12,000."

"This isn't the Redwoods," said Vic.

"There's a burl black market on the internet," Seeley raved. "These two could be part of it."

"The Amish don't have the internet," Vic said.

"They don't have cars, either, but how'd they get here?"

"We were dropped off," Mr. Stoltzfus politely interjected. "Our community has a driving service."

The sobriety of his explanation, along with the eager yet docile look on his son's face, gave Mr. Stoltzfus all the credibility he needed.

"Get out of the way," Connie said to the landscaper. "The longer you stand there, the longer I have to wait for my table."

Her head gave two violent pecks, meant to unman Seeley, but they had the reverse effect. He backed up against the burl as if he were hitching himself to it. "They'll have to cut through me first," he said, grubby yet dignified.

Of all the workers, the carpenter saw what was coming. He who had witnessed so much already, who had been on the job since the very beginning, he alone could see the end to the stand-off. He walked over to Seeley and whispered in his ear. Seeley tried to speak but the carpenter silenced him with an emphatic "No!" He placed a hand on Seeley's chest, to corral him, and Seeley listened more closely, letting the old man's words enter him like a charge. When the carpenter knew that he was ready, he led Seeley away and sat him in the grass at the edge of the lawn. Facing the street, Seeley crossed his legs and started tearing up blades of fescue and letting them fall through his fingers. The carpenter stood behind him, one eye on the maple and one eye on Seeley, making sure that if he turned around, he could not see what was happening to the tree.

Though it was a big burl, five feet in diameter, Stoltzfus and his son made short work of it. One straight cut down the back and it fell away cleanly onto its face. The momentum sent it jouncing across the roots to a spot just inches from where Connie was standing. She knelt beside the burl and ran her hand over its surface, brushing aside the sawdust to better see the pattern of knots and whorls. She was trying to reconcile the table in her mind with this raw piece of wood, and gulped when she couldn't.

"It'll look better once the varnish is on, right?" she asked Mr. Stolzfus.

"Yes," he replied. "You can't judge it now. You have to wait until the aniline brings out the shapes. Excuse me."

Connie moved aside as the Amish picked up the burl and carried it to the opposite side of the lawn, a good distance from Seeley and the carpenter. Agreed this was the end of the show, the crowd dispersed. A few of the workers went over to console Seeley; some took to the air-conditioned shells of their trucks and vans. Frank walked alongside Bruce Patton and asked about the replacement part. Bruce said that it was still on its way, but he couldn't say when it would get there, or how long it would take to install once it arrived. You never knew with these newer units; they were tricky. In the Windsor van, his face held close to the puffing vent, Frank listened to a voicemail from Janet Malloy, reminding him that he was scheduled to pick her rug up later that afternoon. Later that afternoon? No, he wouldn't wait until then. He would clean up his tools and go now, before the tree began to bleed.

CHAPTER NINE

In the early eighties, when Frank first started working for his Uncle John, a good chunk of Windsor's business came from a group of customers dubbed the "Summer Rug Gang." These dozen customers, blue bloods who lived in turn-of-the-century Tudors and shingle-style Victorians, owned two sets of rugs: one for the colder months and one for the warmer. The rugs in the first set were antique Orientals and bordered Wiltons, heirlooms that had been in their families for two or three generations. The rugs in the second set were made of straw, and they were kept in the basement until the middle of May, when John and Frank would come out and make the switch, taking up the wool and putting down the flax. They would bring the lavish winter rugs—eight or nine at a time depending on the size of the house—back to the plant in Folcroft, where they would clean and store them until the first cold of fall.

The Summer Rug Gang believed that this practice, also inherited, was a boon to their health and comfort. Dust and allergens did not cling to the straw, and the rooms breathed more without the heavy coverings. It had surely been a help to Windsor, a perennial source of income that could always be relied on when other parts of the business were slow. Uncle John often said how lucky they were to be rug men in the Delaware Valley, so close to the Main Line and all its old ways, all its old money. But those old ways and that old money belonged to old people, and they eventually grew older and died, and with them went their carpets, their customs, and their business. Only one member of the original Summer Rug Gang remained, and that was Mrs. Janet Malloy.

"I'm still here," she said to Frank, leading him back to the den. "I haven't gone to another dimension or galaxy . . . yet."

Janet had bright blue eyes and shoulder-length, grayish-blonde hair. Over six feet tall, she had been an avid tennis player for most of her adult life, and you could see it in the sweep of her limbs as she jaunted from room to room. She spoke in a high-toned, aristocratic voice, but had a way of sounding sophisticated without being condescending. Janet had always been the kindest and most self-possessed of the Summer Rug Gang, even after her husband Daniel died from a heart attack one month shy of their fiftieth wedding anniversary. Frank hoped that being in her presence—to say nothing of her functional air-conditioning—might somehow stop the leeching of his own dwindling resolve.

Janet's den was a sunless, wood-paneled room at the back of the house where she liked to read *The New Yorker* and talk on the phone with her sister in Connecticut. She switched on a pair of Tiffany lamps, illuminating the sofa, the leather chest that served as a coffee table, and the 4' × 6' Herez with a fist-sized hole in the corner. Frank set down the ice water that Janet had poured for him and slowly circled the rug, looking for any other disruptions in the pile. He came back to the hole, a grot in the rug's turtle and rosette border, and scuffed it once with his sneaker to agitate the fibers. "Has it recently gotten bigger?" he asked.

"I'd say it has," Janet reflected. "I spent two weeks with my oldest son and his family, and when I came back about a month ago it was definitely bigger."

Frank squatted over the hole and picked through the fibers, rubbing them between his fingers, pulling them apart. "Have you seen any moths flying around?" he asked. "Not the ones you find outside, but the tiny beige ones."

"Is that what you think it is: moths?"

Frank nodded. "There's no activity in here now, but the larvae were plenty busy before they cocooned."

"This is the only rug I don't swap out," Janet frowned. "It belonged to Daniel's parents. Is there anything you can do to save it?"

Frank studied the stiff and angular floral design of the Herez, its good, heavy nap. He would never be able to assume their likeness in a patch. His best would be little more than a gross facsimile, roughly sewn into place and drawn with fabric markers nowhere near the pigmentation of the original dyes. Then he had a thought. "What would you say to replacing it?" he asked.

Janet looked at him askance. "With what?"

"A Kirman. I had one come into my shop last Friday. The colors are different, but it's the same size. A guy I do business with picked it up at an estate sale, and he's trying to move it."

"How much is he asking?"

"I'm not sure, but I can call him and find out. It's a beautiful piece, one of the nicer Kirmans I've seen in a while."

"I trust you, Frank, as I always have. I just don't know if I'll like it without seeing it first. You understand."

"Absolutely."

"Would you mind bringing it out so I can have a look at it in the room? Perhaps tomorrow or Friday if either of those days fits your schedule."

Frank could've laughed when Janet said "schedule," but he merely grinned and sipped his water. She knew nothing of his larger turmoil, and he wasn't about to tell her. She had always praised his work and respected his opinion. Her favorite word to describe him was "superb," and he didn't want to present anything to the contrary.

"I might be able to swing by on Friday," he said. "Midmorning."

He slid the chest aside and rolled up the Herez. Janet walked him out and they stood together on the wraparound porch, talking about the retirement community where she was looking to buy a townhouse. She said that some of her friends had moved there and they seemed very happy.

"It would be a much smaller house," she said, "with not nearly as much stuff. I don't know whether I'd do the straw rugs anymore. There might not be a place to store them."

"I could keep them at my shop," Frank said. "I wouldn't charge you the storage fee."

"That's an idea, but I need to sell this hulk first before I do anything."

"Have you had any offers?"

"Not lately, no. There are people who say they like old houses, but I'm beginning to think that this house might be *too* old. So many of the rooms are cold and dark and drafty. It *scares* people. And another thing: I haven't done any major renovations in probably the last thirty years. This house looks exactly as it did in 1989, and that's not what buyers want. They want the old and the new to coexist, but unless you're on one of those of home remodeling shows that I can't stand, you won't be able to create that. It's unattainable without a decorator, and all those fellows like you, Frank, who are so brilliant with their hands. You know me: Daniel and I always made the interior design choices ourselves, and we got all of our contractor recommendations from friends. That's how we found out about Windsor. The Prestons—you remember the Prestons—they swore by your uncle, and that was way back in the *sixties*. Him, and then you, Frank, especially you, you made the house more livable. The work that you did for Daniel and I always made us feel so comfortable here."

"These days," Frank said, "people want more than that."

"What more could they want?" Janet flared. "I mean, sure, we kept up with the Joneses in our time. We compared ourselves to each other, we held up what we had to what they had, and talked about it on the car ride home. But today's envy is different. It never sleeps."

"And neither do I," said Frank.

"I just hope that they know what they have in you. I just hope that they're treating you right."

Frank hugged Mrs. Malloy and started down the wide porch steps with the rug under his arm.

"What are you going to do with the Herez?" Janet asked.

Frank stopped and turned around. "I planned on throwing it out," he said. "Trash day's tomorrow."

"I wish we could give it a more proper burial," she said.

"I don't want you to dig a hole, but maybe there's something you can do before you put it out on the curb."

"Like last rites?"

"Yes. A few words before it goes up to that great loom in the sky."

Continuing down the steps, Frank remarked, "I may have to get ordained for that."

"I believe you already are," said Janet.

FRANK SAT AT THE DESK in his office, paging through Wallace Jacoby's *Oriental Rugs: A Complete History.* Published in 1954, it was the only source book his uncle had ever owned; he used to refer to it as Windsor's Koran, and believed that everything in it was sacred law. If Jacoby hadn't written about it, then it wasn't worth knowing. John's reverence for the stained and tattered hardcover naturally became his nephew's. Any question that couldn't be answered from experience Frank would put to Jacoby, and so it was with this latest query about the rite of disposal.

Frank leafed and scanned, leafed and scanned, coming to a section entitled, "The Life of a Practical Antique Rug." He read:

> Weavers of ancient Oriental carpets made them for their own use without any intention of selling them. The rug was their floor, their bed, their dining room, their door, and often their partition between rooms. This variety of use, along with the Hamadani's nomadic lifestyle, meant that these carpets had to be durable, able to withstand harsh weather conditions and weeks of travel on donkey or camelback. Many of the older rare rugs, the Ispahans

and Herats, lasted 200 years, some even longer. When a rug became too worn for practical use, the Hamadani would take it out and beat it for a time, thus releasing the "dust" of the man who had woven it. If any part of the rug was salvageable, the remnants would be used as blankets or upholstery for what small pieces of furniture they did own.

Since the hole the grubs had made stretched beyond the rug's border to the field, the only part that Frank could save was the center medallion, a figure of a blue lotus. But he didn't want to cut the medallion out until after the rug had been "dusted." So he dragged the Herez back to the dry room and raised it halfway to the ceiling on one of the long, spiked poles. A few rows behind, Mr. Charleston's Kirman seemed to say, *It's unfortunate what happened to you, but don't get too close. My compassion is no repellent to moths. I pray I haven't offended you.* And the Herez responded, *I understand your concern, and I treasure your politeness. A serious thing is about to happen. I'm glad that you're here with me.*

As Frank was looking for something to beat the Herez with, his cell phone rang. For once it was in his pocket.

"Hello," he answered.

"Hey, Frank. It's Christy. How are you?"

"Two men down and one day behind." Frank began nervously pacing the length of the shop. "Any news?"

"I finally got ahold of Billy's dad. He's flying in on Friday. I also talked to Kyle's mom. I want her to come down here but she refuses. She said she doesn't care if Kyle ever gets out. Said she's not paying one cent of his bail. I guess Billy's dad has to get them both out."

"And when's that?"

Christy hesitated. "Monday morning at the earliest."

Frank gritted his teeth. "That's not doing me any good," he said. "That's not doing me any good at all."

"There's more," said Christy.

"What?"

"The story's going to be in tomorrow's *Daily Times*. My dad's lawyer was down at the police station and he saw a reporter he knows talking to the chief."

"Are they printing their pictures?"

"I have no idea, but I'm sure their names'll be in there, along with the rest of the assholes that got arrested."

Frank stopped pacing a few feet from Norm Kershner's high boy, which had been standing against the wall since Billy had brought it back on Monday afternoon.

"Was Billy just using, or was he selling, too?" Frank asked.

"Billy uses, like everybody," Christy said. "But the thing is he was *finding* people at the bar for Kyle to sell to. Kyle would sit in the car in the parking lot. The undercover agents said Billy was like a middle-man. He'd take four or five people a night out to the car. Tuesday night he took the wrong people and now he's going to jail."

"Is that what your dad's lawyer thinks?"

"Unless he can argue entrapment, but that's a long-shot."

"How much time?"

"Eighteen months. Maybe more. We might be able to get him into a program where he leaves the prison during the day and comes to work with you. You'd just have to agree to it and sign some papers."

Frank stared at the highboy. He could feel his heart beating faster.

"To be honest with you, Christy, I'm not sure if I want him back."

"I don't blame you," she said. "I may not want him back either," and on this last word her voice trembled and broke.

It gnarled Frank to hear her crying, this woman who had done nothing wrong—nothing except fall in love with a fool.

"Let me know if anything changes," he said. "And try to keep it together."

"I will," said Christy. "Bye."

"Bye."

Frank pocketed the phone, still staring at the highboy. His heart was beating even faster now, his veins filling with a great surge of blood, hot, irate. This time he knew he wouldn't be able to fight it down, so he let it overtake him. He rushed to the highboy and stomped on the gimpy leg. It took one true strike and the limb broke off, and the highboy fell with a slap, face-first on the concrete. He picked up the leg by its claw and ball foot and, wielding it like a club, marched back to the Herez. He struck the blue lotus over and over, but he was only able to muster a few small poofs of dust. He went around beating other parts of the rug, unsure whether the ritual was having its desired effect. There didn't seem to be enough dust in the rug to constitute a man's spirit. Maybe Janet's housekeeper had sucked it up in the vacuum, he thought, or maybe the moths had eaten it. There was really no way to tell. He just had to trust Jacoby's research and hope that somewhere in the particles begrudged him, a weaver had come forth.

DINNER THAT NIGHT was one of Donna's specialties: breaded chicken cutlets topped with sharp provolone cheese, broccoli rabe, and roasted red peppers. Frank ate the meal deliberately, pleasuring in the different textures and flavors, chewing each bite until it was small and smooth, a pasty lozenge he mourned having to send down his gullet. The meal tasted better to Frank than it had ever tasted before, and he complimented Donna more than once on its place in the pantheon of dinners. And he was elated to report that he hadn't found one cat hair in his food. That, he declared, was something to celebrate.

Donna sensed something unusual in Frank's overly generous review, in the loose way that he held his utensils, the delight in his eyes as he swigged his beer. He was like a child, or like a man recovering from a grave accident, coming out of a fog to the giddiness of life. She asked him about his day, and he said nothing, just continued with the blissful exercise of eating. When she pressed him again, Frank put down his fork and looked at her. The joy left his eyes and his face went dark; it was as if a shadow had fallen over him, obscuring his features.

Seeing the change her question had wrought, Donna took his stubbly cheek in her hand. Frank caved at her touch, revealing everything that had happened that day: the trip to see Gord, the news about Billy, his confrontation with Vic, the torment of the loft, Seeley and the burl, Janet Malloy's moth-eaten Herez. With each new turn of the story, Donna drew herself closer to him, so that by the end of Frank's confession she was holding him in her arms, caressing his short, black hair and kissing him on the forehead.

She thought he felt brittle in her arms, as though she might snap him were she to squeeze a little harder. Had she ever seen him this bad? Had the job ever been this cruel to him? Surely it had, but Donna couldn't remember when, or else she had long ago chased the details from her mind. She released him and watched as he finished the rest of his dinner. He was just as deliberate as before, but without the boyish wonder.

Earlier that day, Donna had called Dr. Temoyan and he had told her that Frank should be applying hot and cold compresses to the back of his leg once a day. She waited until after Frank had spooned through his bowl of vanilla ice cream and then made him lie on his stomach on the living room floor with two throw pillows propped beneath his chin. She soaked a hand towel with hot water, wrung it out in the kitchen sink, flattened it squarely over his hamstring, and sat beside him watching the Phillies game while the compress did its work. When the towel was no longer warm to the touch, she soaked it in cold water and repeated the rest of the process. A half-dozen times she traveled to the kitchen, alternating between temperatures, pausing once to give Ferdinand a post-prandial treat. As she was lifting away the final compress, she asked Frank how his leg felt. He said that it felt better, that the pain seemed milder, more distant. He was lying, of course, but Donna didn't let on that she knew.

"Can I model my new bathing suit for you?" she asked.

Frank rolled over onto his back. "Yes," he smiled. "I would like that."

They both went upstairs and Frank sat on the bed with his eyes obediently shut while Donna changed into a black one-piece. After adjusting the straps, she gave him the okay to look. He couldn't see her in the dusky room, couldn't make her out clearly, so he reached for the lamp on the dresser and she playfully smacked his hand, telling him the light was fine. He looked her up and down, asked her to turn around, to walk back and forth. She did these things for her husband, embarrassed yet emboldened by his requests. She stood with her back to the window, its drawn blinds fringed with the last of the day's sun, and he gazed upon her stout figure, brave in his lust. He pulled her toward him and her body acquiesced, pliant and soft. She would not deny him his pleasure, and he would not be denied. His hands ranged over her breasts, her back, her waist, her bottom, and here they lingered, squeezing the abundant flesh of her cheeks. He moaned and smiled and shook his head all at the same time. He could not believe that there was something else in this world to hold besides metal and wood, the cold, hard handles of tools. He shuddered, went slack, almost wept in recognition of what this woman was about to give to him. The way was open, and they went together into its old, familiar expanse, she leading him forward, he nudging her on. When they finally got there, to the land of the Great Reprieve, he gripped her by the back of the neck and breathed into her mouth that he loved her, and she parted her legs wider, giving him the last reaches of her, and his reception there numbed him to the pain of his life.

"WHAT ARE YOU going to do?"

Husband and wife lay in bed watching one of Donna's true crime shows. It was a commercial break and Frank was fighting to keep his eyes open. Donna asked him again, louder this time, "What are you going to do?"

Frank opened his eyes fully, and they livened in the glare of the television. "I don't know," he said. "I haven't thought about it."

"Well, maybe you should. You have to go back there tomorrow."

"I don't want to go back."

"I don't want you to either, at least not by yourself."

"If it hadn't been so damn hot, I would've finished the loft. I might've even gotten one of the bedrooms done."

"How were you planning on getting the rugs upstairs? With a crane?"

"I was going to carry them."

"Not on this," she said, poking his leg. "You wouldn't have made it through the front door."

"I would've found a way. I always do."

The show resumed, but they were no longer interested in the problems of strangers. Donna turned on her side, engaging Frank, whose tired hands rested on his stomach.

"Is there somebody on the job site you could ask for help?"

"They're all busy with their own bullshit."

"What about the drifters at Home Depot, the day laborers?"

"They don't let guys do that anymore. They were beating each other up in the parking lot. Too many dogs, not enough scraps."

Donna hesitated, then said, "Maybe if Paul wasn't on vacation—"

Frank cut her off with a sharp, cynical laugh.

"What?!" said Donna. "If he knew you were desperate . . ."

"I'm not desperate."

"Yes, you are. Did you not see yourself at dinner?"

"No," said Frank, "I only saw you." And he kissed her on the cheek.

"I'm serious, Frank."

"I can tell."

He rolled over so that he was facing the wall. Donna switched off the television and the room went silent and dark.

"What would John do?" she asked.

"He never would've found himself in this position."

"Why not?"

"Because he had me."

CHAPTER TEN

Frank bought a coffee and Thursday's *Daily Times* from the convenience store up the street from his shop. Sipping the hot coffee, the newspaper unfolded on the steering wheel of his van, he read the story on page 3:

Drug Crackdown Rocks Upper Darby

Two rookie police officers posing as a young couple were key to an undercover operation that identified 15 alleged drug dealers out of several local bars.

Officers Maria Tikos and Shawn Reneiri stood beside Police Chief Richard Senkow and Delaware County District Attorney P. Michael Brown at the Upper Darby War Memorial Wednesday afternoon to announce the successful culmination of the four-month-long detail known as "Operation Bootlegger."

The name stems from Bootlegger's Bar, where most of the drug deals took place, officials said.

As a result of the investigation, 23 arrest warrants have been issued for 15 people who face charges of drug possession with the intent to deliver and other related offenses.

The drugs involved include prescription pills, methamphetamine, cocaine, marijuana, and LSD.

Frank continued reading, smarting when he got to the list of suspects' names. (Fortunately, the article's only picture was of Chief Senkow in front of the war memorial.) He ran through all the people working the Silberstein job and concluded that the only person who knew Billy and Kyle by name was Elaine George. She was not a frequent reader of the *Times* (she said it was a rag), but since blue-collar guys favored it over the *Inquirer*, which leaned left, there was always a copy of it lying around, and Elaine wasn't above picking it up and reading a story or two. I'd rather tell her myself, thought Frank, than have her find out that way. If she hears it from me, maybe I can contain it, maybe it doesn't get to Connie and Vic as fast. But before he could tell her anything, he needed to find a warm body— and fast.

The first person he called was Mike Ianizzi, a knock-about friend of Paul's who, in the past, had lent Frank a hand when he needed some extra muscle. It was a quarter past eight, and Frank doubted whether Mike was even awake. To his relief, Mike answered, but he told Frank that he was building a deck with his brother-in-law and wouldn't be available until the middle of next week. Frank made it clear that he needed him *now*. Mike apologized, but he couldn't bail on family. Frank said he understood. Strike one.

Next he called the drunk Al Fermonte. Al used to live across the street from Frank's uncle, and John would bring him out on big jobs to help with the grunt work. This was ten years ago, and Frank didn't even know if Al was at the same number. The phone rang several times before Al's wife picked up—his *ex*-wife, as Frank came to find out. They had gotten a divorce after Al had fallen off

a ladder and broken his pelvis. Son of a bitch took too long
to recover, so she ended it. He was hooked on painkillers,
living in an apartment above Mickey's Tavern, collecting disability. She could give him his number if he really
wanted to talk to him. Frank said not to worry about it.
Strike two.

Then, not wanting it to come to this, he walked the two
blocks to the halfway house on Township Line. When
he was in a jam about six months ago, he had recruited
two recovering addicts for a week's worth of labor. They
weren't very skilled with their hands, and the one spent
most of his time in the bathroom, but they were thankful to have the work, and it felt good for Frank to give it to
them. There were two counselors at the halfway house, a
man and a woman. When Frank opened the door to the
facility, the woman was sitting at a desk in the reception
area, eating a breakfast sandwich. She remembered Frank
from the last time he had been there and wished she could
recommend someone, but all the house members were on
a day trip to the shore and weren't expected back until
after dinner. She took Frank's number and said she'd call
him tomorrow morning if anyone was interested in working. Strike three.

The office phone was ringing when he got back to the
warehouse. He checked the Caller ID: Google Marketplace. Rolling his eyes, Frank let the machine answer, and
there was that sultry voice again: "Hello, Mr. Renzetti,
this is Amanda, and I want you to know that you have just
one day left to reserve your spot in the Marketplace. If you
don't act now, you'll lose—"

Frank picked up the phone. "Amanda," he said, and it
came out as both a question and a statement.

"Yes," she said, recovering from the interruption. "Is this Frank Renzetti?"

"Yes, this is him."

"Mr. Renzetti, I've been trying to reach you for the past two weeks about joining the Google Marketplace. It's so nice to finally hear your voice. Do you have a few minutes to talk?"

"I don't want to join the Marketplace," he said. "Take me off your list."

"Is there a specific reason *why* you don't want to join?"

"I've been doing this for a long time, and I've never needed advertising to drive my business."

"Then how do people find out about your services?"

"The old-fashioned way," said Frank. "Word-of-mouth."

"I see." After a short, respectful pause: "What if I told you that in five years that word wouldn't be in people's mouths anymore. It would strictly be on their smart-phones."

"I may not be doing this in five years, so what difference does it make?"

"Are you thinking of retiring?"

"Yeah. Tomorrow."

Amanda dropped the commercial affect from her voice. She was speaking to Frank as a person now, not as a sales-woman. "Is there something I can do for you?" she asked.

"No," said Frank, "unless you can deliver an able-bodied man to my warehouse in the next thirty minutes. Mine happens to be in jail."

"I'm afraid I can't send you a man, but I can tell you where to find one."

Frank began doodling on his planner. "If you say the internet, I'm going to hang up."

"It's not the internet. It's Fat Morty."

Morty Kabrinsky, known to the buying public as Fat Morty, was southeastern Pennsylvania's most notorious purveyor of cut-rate carpet. He specialized in closeouts, odd lots, and overruns, charging next to nothing for the materials but then gouging customers on the installation, which was usually performed by a crew of poorly trained rejects. Along with Loman's and Carpet Cavalry, Fat Morty's was on Frank's short list of local industry cankers, the outfits responsible for keeping alive the story of Vic's stereotypical low-life. They were the ones who fed the Ape, housed him and clothed him, and they made Frank look bad simply by existing.

"Fat Morty's is six miles away from you," Amanda said. "They employ twenty people, and some are sub-contractors who work on loan from the company."

"Thanks," said Frank, "but I've been humiliated enough this week."

"You're just asking for a rental. There's no shame in that."

"Morty's a shyster, always has been, but I guess that doesn't come up on your computer screen."

Frank stopped doodling. His leg was throbbing and he thought that a change in position might bring some relief. He stood and the phone's tangled cord dragged the receiver across the desk.

"Frank?" said Amanda. "Are you still there?"

For a few seconds, Frank didn't say anything. He was waiting to see how the pain would respond. It seemed to have gotten worse. He wanted to break something.

"Why are you pushing Morty on me?" he asked. "Is he a member of the Marketplace?"

"Yes," said Amanda, some of the decorum returning to her voice, "but that's not why I think you should go to him."

Frank fell silent again, waiting.

"Mr. Renzetti," leveled Amanda, "I cover the entire Delaware Valley, and Windsor Carpets is one of the only small businesses in the area to not claim its stake in the Marketplace. I understand that you're set in your ways, and that you may never decide to join, but I want to make available to you one of the perks of membership, and that's connecting you with peers in the field. As hard as it might be for you, I don't want you to look at Fat Morty's as your competition, but as a venue for shared knowledge and resources. You don't strike me as the kind of guy who needs any more knowledge. I can tell that just from talking to you. But you are someone who needs resources, *human* resources, and Fat Morty's has them to give. If you put aside your negative thoughts about the proprietor, you might be able to find a solution to your problem."

Frank sat back down and looked at the doodle on the edge of his planner. It resembled the topaz ball on Connie's newel post. It even had the same pattern of waves and swirls. As he spoke, he drew a square around the sphere, the four sides touching the four convexities.

"I like you," he said.

"Excuse me?" said Amanda.

"I like your voice. I listen to your messages all the way through to the end."

"Then how come you've never called me back?"

"I guess I was playing hard to get."

On Amanda's end of the line, Frank could hear the background babble of the other telemarketers, remind-

ing him that this call was an official communication, and
that everything was being recorded. If Amanda's superi-
ors happened to listen back to it for quality control, she
would likely be disciplined for her indirect approach. She
might even lose her job. Frank suddenly felt guilty for taking advantage of her soft touch. They had both been far
too human.

"I have to go," he told her. "Thanks for the suggestion."

"Are you going to take it?" she asked.

Frank didn't answer, though he asked again to have
Windsor's name removed from the list, to which she cor-
dially agreed. With a final few punishable words, she
hung up.

Much later, thinking back on this moment, Frank would
remember nothing of the argument he had with himself in the office, or the rush-hour traffic he sat through
on West Chester Pike, or the ten minutes he spent in Fat
Morty's parking lot, unable to extricate himself from the
van. What he would recall most vividly was the image
of a young, brown-skinned man crisscrossing Morty's
warehouse in a bright orange forklift. Even before he
spoke to Morty, who was not nearly as fat as advertised,
Frank knew that—among the four or five guys scram-
bling about the floor—this would be the man subbed out
to him, a muchacho, a bad hombre, and thus forbidden on
Vic Satrapini's job site. As he handed Morty a check for
$100, the swindler's daily sub-contracting fee, it occurred
to Frank that he was ransoming his principles for someone who couldn't even show his face at the door.

"Are you sure you don't have anybody else you can
spare?" he asked.

They were standing by a small wooden podium, just

inside the mouth of the great warehouse, with its ceiling-high racks of low-grade carpet and coils of urethane pad.

"Nope," said Morty, holding the check up to the sunlight and squinting at it like a banker. "He's all I've got today."

"Any specific time you want him back?"

"You keep him as long as you want. Just know we close at six. You're any later than that, just drop him off at the nearest bus stop. He knows the schedules."

"What's his name?"

"Edgar. He's from El Salvador . . . I think."

"Is his English any good?"

Morty folded the check and shot it into the breast pocket of his floral-print button-down. "You're not hiring him for his command of the language, are you?"

"No," said Frank uneasily, "I guess I'm not."

"He understands what you're saying," offered Morty, "but he doesn't talk much himself, at least not to me."

He turned into the gloom of the warehouse, mumbled something to Edgar, and disappeared behind a scuffed metal door. The laborer, a smile upon his broad, open face, jogged over to Frank and reached out his hand. He was thickset but not short, with prickly black hair and a sprig of dark mustache. He looked to be in his mid-twenties, though his hand, as Frank shook it in greeting, felt like that of an older man, rough and hard and strong. And— Frank didn't know how else to explain it—wise somehow, and confident, as if that hand had matured faster than the rest of him, and now acted without hesitation or fore-thought, the ambassador of all his experience.

Driving to Heatherstone, Frank warned Edgar about Vic, "the Big Guy," he called him. He paraphrased the story of the stolen golf clubs, and impressed upon Edgar the need to be careful in how he came and went. "The less people that see you, the better," he said.

Edgar nodded. "Invisible," he said.

"Yes," said Frank, "invisible."

Edgar nodded again. "I can do that. I have lots of practice."

"I bet you do."

Frank parked on the street, at the end of a long line of work vehicles, and asked Edgar to wait in the van. He left the radio on and the windows down and cut across the front lawn. He noted the maple's day-old wound, the yellow meat wetted with sap, the bark below it stained from the flow, and he thought of Seeley and the weight of his heart this day. Once inside the house, Frank privately celebrated the return of the air-conditioning. His plan, however it came together, would not take shape in miserable sweat. Bruce Patton was to thank for that.

He found Elaine standing by herself in the sanctuary. Closing the door to the blue-padded room, he apologized for leaving early the day before, and then, in a solemn whisper that made Elaine blanch, he explained the absence of Billy and Kyle, and told her about their temporary replacement. "Believe me, I didn't want to have to bring him," he said, "but I'm holding the ass-end here, and nobody seems to want to hold the other one."

Elaine checked her slender gold watch. "Vic usually gets here at ten. That gives you about a half-hour."

"I just need to bring up the materials," Frank said, "and then we can stay in the bedrooms for the rest of the day."

"Do you really expect Vic not to go up there? It's his instinct to roam."

"Maybe you can occupy him."

"All day?"

"Isn't there somewhere you can take him, something you can do?"

Elaine adjusted her red-framed glasses, scrunched the ball of her chin in thought. "He and Connie are supposed to go look at flagstone tomorrow," she said. "I might be able to talk them into going today, but it would only be for a couple of hours."

Frank stepped toward her, and the sanctuary's floor-boards creaked with his weight. "Two o'clock," he said, chopping his palm. "Keep him off my back until two o'clock."

Elaine sighed, shook her head. "This is crazy," she said. "Even if Vic doesn't see him, somebody else will."

"And if they ask about him, I'll say that he's legal."

"They won't believe you. They'll tell him."

"No they won't. They don't like him enough to tell him."

"If he finds out," said Elaine, her face turning yet paler, "he'll call ICE. He'll have the poor guy deported. He's sick like that."

Frank saw that he was losing her, her faith submitting to the most tragic of futures. The demons of our own sur-mising are always the hardest to exorcize. Frank had been successful in banishing his; he would not permit Elaine, who held more influence than he ever could, to be spooked by hers. He needed her—they needed each other: elegance and utility, the T-pin and the T-square. Taking another step toward her, he rested a hand on both her shoulders and gently squeezed. It was the first time in their six-year relationship that he had ever touched her.

"Do you want me to finish on time?" he asked.

She nodded.

"Do you want me to deliver the rug for this room by tomorrow morning, before the furniture comes? Does *Connie* want that?"

"Yes."

Frank lowered his head so that his eyes were level with hers. "Then help me get this guy across the border."

Elaine smiled at his simple joke, and some of the color returned to her cheeks.

Frank let his hands fall to his sides. "I'm going to the shore tomorrow to see my grandson," he said, "and I don't want this job in front of me. I want it behind me."

Elaine said that she understood, that it's what she wanted, too, despite the contractors' gossip. She had had to turn down several jobs since agreeing to help Connie with the renovation. Dunwoody Lane was taking up all her time, all her energy. She wanted it be over as much as anyone, maybe even more. She was closest to Connie, the channel for her anger and anxiety, and that closeness had become a burden—a lucrative one, surely, but a burden nonetheless. She hadn't seen her daughter in over a week, and pretty soon she would be leaving for Cornell. They hadn't even bought the décor for her dorm room yet. Frank didn't need to say another word about it. She knew exactly what he was saying.

As they were walking through the room's double doors together, shoulder-to-shoulder, Elaine gave him directions to the Pennsport docks, where he was supposed to be picking up the sanctuary rug, which had arrived only yesterday from China. "The distribution center closes at six," she said. "The rug's in Lot 17B. They're keeping it next to the receiving office. Remember, the sidemark on the packaging is Timeless Peacock."

"What time is the furniture getting here tomorrow?" Frank asked.

"Eight a.m.," she said. "We're their first stop of the day."

"I'll be here at 7:30," Frank said.

"You better be. You owe me."

CHAPTER ELEVEN

The men were fast about it, but they could only be so stealthy using the front door, the easiest and most popular point of access. They carried the rug and pad to the second-floor hallway, making a half-dozen trips. Those who would be witnesses glanced twice at Edgar and muttered amongst themselves. Frank didn't see anyone taking pictures of Edgar, but to reduce the risk of this happening, he sent him upstairs to finish padding the loft. He didn't give him any specific instructions, trusting that Morty had taught him enough to apply a layer of felt.

Frank began moving small pieces of furniture from Rachel's bedroom into the adjoining Jack and Jill bathroom. Every few minutes he would stop and look out the window for Vic's pickup, panning the street from east to west and back again. As he was clearing the top of Rachel's desk, he heard a truck door slam and froze where he stood, a box of colored pencils clutched in his hand. He went to the window and saw Vic lumbering up the path, but, to his great relief, the ball-breaker only made it halfway before Elaine and Connie met him coming in the opposite direction. The trio spoke briefly, Vic standing there like a monument the two women were visiting. Then, quite suddenly, with the crafty Elaine shooing them along, they boarded Connie's Yukon and were off to ponder flagstone.

Frank watched them drive away, and the morning opened up like a second dawn. The urgency to move in that provisional freedom was like nothing he had felt in years. He prayed it would last.

Edgar padded the loft and came down to help Frank with the larger pieces of bedroom furniture, the desks and the dressers, armoires and divans. Because Edgar worked quickly and quietly, because he wasn't in the habit of always checking his phone, they emptied Rachel's room, Miranda's room, and the guest room in less time than it would've taken the Bootleggers to empty just one of them. They packed the furniture as tightly as they could into the master bedroom, using every inch of floor space, even sliding a few items into the walk-in closet. Frank knew that Connie wouldn't be happy about this: the feet of wood and metal were going to leave dents in the new carpet. But there was nowhere else to put the furniture, and really, what were dents compared to the holes—no, craters—Vic would leave if he caught Edgar in the house? Between Vic's wrath and Connie's mania, the choice was easy for Frank. If dents could save him from the former, then let there be dents. They could be coaxed out with warm water and the blunt end of a scrub brush. As for the alternative, he was not so sure.

Frank and Edgar took up the ends of the rug for the loft and kinked the roll into a V shape. They hoofed it up the narrow stairway and let the ends flop to the floor. Whenever Frank bearhugged a carpet like this, its latex backing grated his forearms. He looked at them, and the skin was red and chafed. It wasn't painful, just uncomfortable. As they unrolled the rug with stiff nudges of the toe, Frank glanced over to see whether the same thing had happened to Edgar, but his brown skin concealed any abrasion. Edgar was wearing a look of contentment, a faint smile that seemed to never leave his lips. Either he was happy in his work, or he was impervious to it. Whichever it was, Frank envied him.

Edgar fetched a kicker, a tuck knife, and a blade from the tool box and began securing the far-left corner of the carpet. Frank got his own tools and joined Edgar on the floor. He told him that he wanted the rug stretched first in the length and then in the width, using hand gestures to illustrate. Edgar nodded dramatically, pushing out his bottom lip and crinkling his brow. It looked to Frank like he was mocking him. He stared at Edgar. This guy might know *what* to do, he thought, but let's see if he knows *how*.

It was rare for Frank to allow someone else to take the lead. When installing a carpet, when doing anything mechanical at all, he was the one to dictate the pace, he was the one to establish a rhythm. It felt strange, then, to be following behind Edgar, odd to be in the train of another man's work. How long had it been since Frank had played the second squirrel? Not since the days of his apprenticeship, and that had been under a true master, an Ace. This was a guy he had picked up at Fat Morty's on a last-minute recommendation from a sexy-voiced telemarketer. How could he possibly be any good? But he was— he was *very* good. Swift yet precise, keen yet patient, he scurried about the loft and not a single move was wasted. The more Frank watched him the more he became convinced that Edgar had learned the trade *before* his time at Morty's, probably from a family member. There was too much trust in his hands, too much balance in his body for him to have been taught by someone who didn't love him and didn't know that someday he would use the skill to earn his daily bread. Beyond the simple application of goods, Edgar demonstrated a spirit, a presence of memory, and his every boot of the kicker, his every turn of the blade, seemed to honor that memory, as though the carpet was a plane upon which that spirit walked, proudly, into the future.

They breezed through the loft and started ripping up the bedrooms. Frank hauled the old pad and carpet out to the curb, something he hadn't done in years. On one of his trips back up the main stairs he paused on the bottom step and looked at the glass finial. He touched its rounded surface and it felt as cold as it did on Monday morning, colder even. He imagined that if he stared into it long enough its dark clouds would break and show him a glimmer of things to come. But Frank decided that he didn't want to see that destiny—the one swimming in the Silberstein eye. For what he saw might chase him from the spot, and he couldn't leave now, this close to the end. No, any portent would arise from his own divination. That way he could ensure that this house would not be in it, and therefore he would not be in this house. Best to be your own augur in times like these.

Edgar worked Rachel's room with the door closed while Frank worked the guest room. They didn't break for lunch; it would've only slowed them down. The back of Frank's leg was aflame, had been since the call with Amanda, but there was nothing he could do about it, so he just

kept going. Edgar finished before him and went directly
to Miranda's room, doubling up the rug and shouldering
it by himself. Frank eventually joined him, and to fill the
air between them he whistled a high, happy tune. When it
flagged, or when Frank tired of its repetition, Edgar would
pick up the melody, adding his own strain before giving it
back to Frank anew. This became the soundtrack to their
wordless crawl, the music of branded knees. It lasted until
the final section of Beachfront Vista had been tucked
behind the tackless, and they were sitting across from
each other with their backs against the wall, hands crumpled in their laps, chests rising and falling. Frank looked at
Edgar and almost laughed.

"Thank you," he said.

"You're welcome," said Edgar.

"Who taught you?" Frank asked.

"My brother, Armando," Edgar said. "He started a business and it was good, but then his wife had a baby. He
went back."

"To El Salvador?"

"Yeah. The city where I'm from: San Miguel."

Frank stood and Edgar all but mirrored him.

"Your brother was a good teacher," Frank said.

Edgar made that mocking gesture again. "I'm a good
student," he said.

And this time Frank did laugh, and there was no part
of him in which it did not resound, healthy and deep and
true. Edgar laughed with him, and they were loud enough
that Frank almost missed his phone going off. It was resting on Miranda's window sill beside a box of pad staples. He flicked it open and read a short text from Elaine:
"Be there in 15 mins." Man, she likes cutting it close, he

thought, and issued Edgar the "hurry-up" sign, a blurred winding of his hand, and thumbed Elaine a response: "Upstairs offlimits do best to keep him away."

They bagged up the leavings and vacuumed the carpet and stationed the furniture where they thought they remembered it going. Rachel's room gave them the most trouble, as that had been the first one they emptied. Their minds—pushed ever forward by Vic's impending return—just couldn't travel back that far. Did her desk go by the window or next to the bathroom door? Which lamp went on her nightstand and which on her chest of drawers? What about the picture of Rachel and her friends at the aquarium, an image of a great white shark filling the background, ready to devour them? Where did that go? Frank first tried it on the desk, then on the nightstand, then on the console table beneath the mirror. Nothing looked right. He wished that Elaine George had been with them. She would've known where the picture went—where *everything* went, and how to place it just so. At a loss, Frank handed the picture to Edgar, and he was staring at it quizzically, having never before seen anything like it, these giddy girls and this deadly shark, when the front door opened and the gang pulsed in. Not just the Renovation Complex, but Rachel and Miranda, too, home early from camp and asking to see their new carpet.

Edgar flung the picture on the bed as if it had just burnt him. In a flash of cunning, Frank clawed him by the shoulders and shoved him down the hall into Connie's bedroom. He opened the first window on the far wall and made Edgar climb out onto the scaffolding that the stone masons had still not broken down. The structure swayed with Edgar's weight, and he gripped the rusty supports.

"Stay here until I come get you," said Frank.

Edgar nodded, his constant half-smile now a grimace.

Frank closed the window, drew the blinds, and jogged to the top of the stairs, composing himself to greet the herd. But they had stalled in the foyer. Something was wrong. Rachel and Miranda wanted to know where the dog was. Why hadn't he come out to see them?

"He's probably sleeping," said Connie.

"He always gets excited when we come home," said Rachel, "even when he's sleeping. He *hears* us."

Vic looked up at Frank, his chin like an arrow aimed at Frank's chest. "Is he up there?"

"No," said Frank. "I haven't seen him all day."

One of the painters slumped through the front door with his head down, looking like all he wanted in the world was to be left alone. Connie accosted him about the dog, and he told them that P.J. had been scratching at the back door and Seeley had let him out.

"How long ago was this?" Connie asked.

"About an hour," the painter said.

Rachel screamed and Miranda dropped her violin case and the younger sister pushed the older sister out the rear foyer door, the adults just a few paces behind.

"I killed his tree," Connie raved, "now he's trying to kill my dog. He can't last ten minutes in this heat."

When he knew that they were safely outside, Frank ducked back into the master bedroom. He opened the window and softly called Edgar's name, but he did not answer. Frank lifted the screen and stuck his head out: the top plank was deserted. Bracing himself against the window frame, he stepped onto the scaffolding and peered down the front and two sides for a glimpse of Edgar, a hand or a foot, that fright of black hair, but the lower levels were just as empty as the top one. Save for the shunting caused by Frank's cautious steps, the scaffolding was eerily still. It was as though Edgar had disappeared, or, as though he had never been, his time at Windsor the current of a dream that Frank was just now waking up from.

He walked to the edge of the scaffolding, where the vista took in much of the Silberstein's back yard and all of their neighbor's to the right. Connie's yard, which had as its primary attractions an in-ground pool, a volleyball net, and a trampoline, was enclosed on three sides by a ten-foot-high white wooden fence that one could neither look through nor over. The search party was spread out like the fingers of a trembling hand, calling P.J.'s name, whistling and clapping. They hadn't found him yet, and Rachel was crying. Connie yelled at her to stop, and Miranda yelled at her mother, and then the three of them were arguing loudly, and Vic and Elaine trooped over and that shaking hand bunched into a fist. It clenched and turned red, clenched and turned red, and the fist would've gone on beating itself up had Seeley not strolled onto the pool deck with a freshly potted begonia. The fist wheeled around and jabbed at Seeley, and he staggered back and almost fell into the pool. He regained his balance and pointed to the gate on the side of the house. The gate swung into the shaded passage above which Frank was standing and led to the front yard. The party profaned Seeley and punched through the gate. Their stampede shook the scaffolding and Frank had to stifle a cry as he groped for the rail with both hands.

A lawnmower started up a few houses over. Frank's eyes jumped to the sound, and then slid back in a kind of dragline, catching on the neighbor's shed, which he could see diagonally from his lookout. He sensed movement there; not inside, but behind it, a troubling of the crepe myrtle overhanging its roof. He watched, and moments later Edgar emerged from the shade with P.J. cradled in his arms. The dog's legs were spread and he was panting, his belly black with mulch. The next-door neighbor—the power-walker with the pink visor—rushed out of her back door to confront Edgar, but he paid her no mind. He swept P.J. along the hedge, his head turned toward the street.

"Edgar," Frank said twice, but it was more for himself than anything else, not loud enough to succeed the hum of the mower or the cicadas boring into the air with their muggy lasers. No, he had called Edgar's name so that he could tell himself later that he had done *some*thing, that he hadn't been as lost or as weak as he truly was, the whole damn thing hadn't gotten away from him, he was still holding the sheet.

Inside, he rounded up the tools and latched them away in their boxes. He carried the boxes down to the foyer and went back upstairs to collect the marginalia: the small square, long straight edge, unused tackless, trash bags, radio, broom and dustpan—the stuff that Kyle usually handled at the end of a long job when Frank could do little more than breathe. He was no less tired now, but he welcomed the chore as a distraction from what he feared was happening outside (Vic pinning Edgar to the tail of his truck, interrogating him, dialing the police), and from what he feared was going to happen to him. How would he be punished for breaking Satrapini's Law? Blacklisted from other jobs where Vic was GC? Refused payment? Elaine thought that Vic was crazy, but what about Connie?

She and Vic seemed chummy, even flirtatious at times. How did *she* feel about him? She was the one signing Frank's check. In the end, Connie's heart mattered most, what little of it there was beneath that baggy black tunic.

The front door opened and once more the foyer crackled with their entrance, relief and joy in the voices of the children, exhaustion and bemusement on the faces of the adults. And pulling them up the stairs like a mushing sleigh dog was the miraculously restored P.J. Frank couldn't believe what he was seeing. Where had this energy come from, when not ten minutes before P.J. lay gasping in Edgar's arms? They followed close behind the dog, except for Elaine. She motioned for Frank to come outside with her. They stood between the fluted columns and she told him what had happened, the whole time fighting down a smile with her bulging, brown eyes. At the best part, she almost lost it.

"So he gives the dog to Rachel," she said, "and Vic gets right in his face and asks him who he is."

"And what did he tell him?" Frank asked.

"He says, 'I'm the invisible man,' and he walks away."

"And what did Vic do?"

"Nothing. He just stood there like an oaf."

"Where's Edgar now?"

"Still walking."

They looked eastward and saw him bopping up Dunwoody Lane with his hands in his back pockets, continuously kicking a rock a few feet ahead of him, just a man passing from here to there.

"I have to get him," said Frank.

He thanked Elaine, and she reminded him of the debt he owed her. He loaded the van and left before Connie and

Vic had even come downstairs. He knew that this was unprofessional, and that he would probably hear about it tomorrow, but he didn't feel like listening to their nit-picking, or, for that matter, their praise, not with Edgar out there walking, mapping a route to the nearest bus stop.

CHAPTER TWELVE

Since they had skipped lunch, both of them were starving, so they picked up Wendy's on their way to the docks. Edgar insisted on paying his share, but Frank wouldn't allow it. He bought him his meal, and when Edgar told him that he had never tried a Frosty before, Frank pulled back around to the drive-thru and ordered two large Frosties, one for Edgar and one for himself.

"You'll like it," he said, handing Edgar the tall cup of chocolate soft serve, "but it might go right through you."

As they neared Pennsport, Frank asked Edgar about the dog. He was curious: how had P.J. gotten into the neighbor's back yard, him so small and that fence so big?

"Underneath," said Edgar. "He dug a tunnel. In the flower bed. The dirt was behind him in a pile. All those eyes and no one saw it."

Edgar's first instinct was to stay put, not let himself be seen, as Frank had ordered, but the dog could barely walk after he had emerged on the other side of the fence. Edgar said he looked like a "new dog, a puppy dog," one that doesn't know where to go or what to do. He thought

P.J. must have chosen the spot behind the shed to either be sick or die. So he climbed down and went to him.

"Elaine, the woman with the curly hair and glasses, told me what you said to Vic."

"The Big Guy?"

"Yeah. The one I warned you about."

"He looked at the dog, he looked at me, and his eyes didn't change. He hated us both—the dog for getting away and me for finding him."

Edgar scraped the bottom of his cup and scooped the last bit of Frosty into his mouth. He seemed sad to have reached the end of it. He licked his spoon ceremoniously, and rather than drop it inside the cup, as most everyone did, he held onto it as though it were a souvenir, dessert's memory in plastic.

"I was afraid he wouldn't let you leave," said Frank.

"The girls wouldn't," said Edgar. "They scared me more than him. Their hugs. They asked me my name first. I didn't tell them, and that's why he asked."

"Did he want to know what you were doing in the neighbor's back yard?"

"He wanted to know everything. I saw in his eyes how much he wanted to know. People like him, you don't say anything to. He is the kind my brother says to always show your back to. It doesn't make you feel less of a man, because they don't think you are one to begin with. You show them your back to save your front. Unless they have a gun and a uniform, you turn and walk away. That is how Armando stayed here so long. He kept the shadows close, even in the day."

"Playing hero to that dog wasn't keeping the shadows close."

"No, it wasn't, but sometimes you have to walk in the sun. You can't hide forever."

"Your brother tell you that too?"

"No, that's what I tell my *hijo*."

The rug was waiting for them just where Elaine had said it would be: outside the receiving office in Lot 17B. A heavyset man came out of the office with a bill of lading. Frank signed it and he and Edgar fought the rug onto the van. It was only a 9 × 12, but it had been shipped inside a thick cardboard tube, which made it awkward to carry. The outside of the tube was smudged with graphite, acquired during its voyage in the dirty hull of a freighter. It left them with black palms and forearms and black stains on their shirts. The heavyset man apologized for the mess, and to even things up he showed them a shortcut off the docks, saving them the trouble of backtracking to the entrance.

At the warehouse, they pried the plastic lid from one end of the tube and, reaching inside, dragged the rug onto the deck. They cut away its burlap casing and rolled it out. Each took a long look at the field but neither said a word. It was made from opulon—Frank knew this on sight. The material gave it a density he thought it didn't deserve, the appearance of wool but without wool's patent. The machines that had spun and dyed it were set to mimic human hands, programmed to be nimble but not too nimble, straight but not too straight. The designs and patterns were perfectly inconsistent, and the colors—turquoise, teal, aquamarine—were weaker in some areas and stronger in others, meant to achieve a chromatic flaw known as abrash. Frank pressed down on the nap with the ball of his foot and the close-tufted fibers did not yield. They had no life to them, no give. He thought, All that money for *this*.

It angered him. When Edgar ran the vacuum over the rug, the coarse pile retained its starch and direction, suggesting that it would always look this way, it would always be static, impermeable, new. Frank wanted to gouge the face with an awl, just to see if he could get through it. Instead he swung down hard on it with his heel.

Edgar stopped the Sanitaire and asked, "A bug?"

"No," Frank said, his leg in shock from the violent action. "I don't like it. It's a wannabe."

"A 'real fake.' That's what Morty would say."

Frank gave a little laugh. "He would know."

Edgar finished vacuuming and they rolled the rug and cinched it with twine at the ends and in the middle. Frank cleared the van of the day's trash and swept the bed with a push broom, making a clean berth for the Timeless Peacock. They walked the rug to the van and it was heavy enough that Frank worried about having to carry it by himself in the morning. Remembering Janet Malloy, he went back to the dry room and dropped both the Kirman and the Herez from their spiked poles. He ran a pile brush over the Kirman to suck up any lint and to give the nap a uniform lift. Charleston sure got lucky finding this one, he thought. The cleaning had erased years from the rug's age, but had done little to diminish its essential character. It still looked like something that had been on the planet for a very long time. He rolled it and tied it and brought it to the van. The Herez he left sitting on the floor.

"What are you doing with that one?" Edgar asked.

"I was going to save the medallion," said Frank, "but I think I'm just going to trash the whole thing. Moths got to it."

Edgar looked at the shabby heirloom with an appraising eye. "Can I have it?" he asked. "My son's stool needs a cushion, for when he eats."

Frank couldn't see why not. Edgar gathered some tools and Frank watched as he flipped the Herez onto its face and cut out the lotus from the back. It was a 2 × 2 square with the blooming blue flower perfectly centered in the height and width. Edgar would apply it to the seat of the stool by making a series of small releases along the carpet's edge and curling the fabric underneath and stapling it in place with a tacker. Frank had seen his Uncle John do it on more than one occasion, though never with the heart of a Herez. The medallion would make a fine upholstery, finer than Edgar's son might ever know. More than just comfortable, more than just warm and well-fed, he would be sitting atop the birth of the world every time he took to it. Vic Satrapini would never be able to get him up there.

Frank looked at his watch: it was almost six o'clock. "Let me give you a ride to Morty's," he said.

Edgar refused the ride, said the bus would be coming soon. He folded the square in half and tucked it under his arm, clamping it there tightly. Whoever might try to take it would have a hard time wrenching it loose. Next to Edgar's wrist Frank could see the handle of the Frosty spoon sticking out the front right pocket of his shorts. As parting gifts, the lotus and the spoon seemed insufficient to Frank. He always carried at least fifty dollars in his wallet. He held out the bills to Edgar.

"No," said Edgar. "You already paid."

"And how much of that are you gonna see?'

"Enough."

Frank extended his hand, urging the money on Edgar. "At least take twenty for the bus and dinner."

"I have a bus pass, and my wife is making dinner."

Edgar was in the street now, walking in the direction of Township Line, where he would catch the 6:15 at the glassed-in shelter on the corner.

"Thank you," said Frank.

Edgar waved with his left hand, for the Herez was in his right, and that would not move until he saw his son. "My life is good," he shouted, and Frank could think of no reason not to believe him.

AFTER HE SHOWERED, Frank dried off and sat naked in the chair beside his dresser. He spread his fingers and looked at the knuckles. They were rough, white bumps, starched and scuffed, their fine wrinkles ground away. He looked at the nail on his left thumb that had never grown back correctly after he had sliced it with a blade years ago when he was new to the trade. A thin vein of keratin ran from one corner of the nail to the other. It was as if a second nail were trying to grow diagonally atop the first. Frank picked at this overlapping ridge whenever it got too thick, though lately he found himself doing it whenever his hands were idle, just to give them something to do. He turned his hands over and looked at the fan of calluses on each palm. The pads were as smooth and as hard as plastic. He struck one with his fingernail and it made a tapping sound that should not emanate from the flesh. He stretched his legs away from his body so that he could see his hairless knees. The skin there was as bleached as the skin of his knuckles, as if the bone were showing through. He drew his legs closer and both knees responded with a clicking sound like the snapping of a button.

Frank didn't know how much longer he had left, how many more years until his body gave out. Five, maybe ten if he was lucky? His Uncle John had made it to 67, but by then he could barely walk. His knees and his back were a constant source of pain. He carried the work in his bones long after he had retired; it haunted him each time he stood, each time he crossed a room. Frank knew that the same thing was in store for his body—there was no way to escape the fact. The same ache that had possessed his uncle would in its turn possess him, and he would have to find a way to live with it. At least now he could fight it down with more work, more pain. This was his remedy: siphon the hurt from one part of his body to another, filling and draining his reservoirs of tolerance. But when there was no more work, no more new pain, he would be left with the old soreness, and it would neither grow nor deplete. It would merely remain, eating at him, for always.

Frank dressed and began packing his suitcase for the trip to Ventnor. Since they were only staying the weekend, he didn't pack much, mostly things for the beach, swim trunks and T-shirts. He went into Paul's room to get the swim fins and stopped when he saw Ferdinand curled up on the bed. The cat had just eaten dinner and it looked like he had found his sleeping quarters for the night. Staring at him, Frank felt a sudden affection for the cat. This hardly ever happened, so he thought he should act on the feeling before it went away.

He sat down with the swim fins in his lap and stroked Ferdinand between the ears. The cat stirred and opened his yellow eyes, turned his head slightly and gave Frank a look that said, "You can keep doing that, but not for much longer. You see what it is I'm trying to do here." Frank had never been very good at interpreting Ferdinand's body language. He went on stroking, remembering what Donna had said once about cats and stress, how petting them can help relieve it. Ferdinand's coat was soft and warm, his breathing a low but steady purr, his "motors," Donna would say. Frank ran a palm along the course of his back, and when he drew his hand away a loose tuft of golden hair clung to his fingers.

For twelve years Frank had been picking these hairs out of his food and lint-rolling them from his shirts and pants. In that time, he had probably unknowingly ingested over a thousand of them. He wondered whether the acid in his stomach broke the hairs down, whether they stayed inside him forever or passed through him with his morning shit. Again, he ran his hand down the length of Ferdinand's back and collected another fine shedding of hair. He kept doing this until he had a rather large clump of fur. This he worked with his fingers, shaping it into a compact ball that he delicately placed on Paul's nightstand. It looked like a small scoop of cookie dough.

"Look what I made out of you," Frank said to Ferdinand. "A sweet."

He packed the swim fins in his suitcase and went downstairs to dinner. Donna was eager to know how things had gone at work. Frank told her about Edgar and how he had saved him despite almost getting him fired. The story—though his own—amazed Frank: it didn't seem possible. Not so much what had happened with Vic and the dog, which was wild enough, but the matter of Edgar himself, the fact that someone of his skill and pedigree even existed. Frank had seen Edgar in the flesh, witnessed him first-hand, and yet he couldn't account for him. He tried to explain his disbelief to Donna, but he only confused her.

"I don't understand," she said. "You don't think he's real because he works at Fat Morty's?"

"No," said Frank, "but that's part of it. It's because he actually knew what he was doing, knew it without knowing, if that makes any sense."

"He kept up with you. That's what you're saying."

"He didn't keep up with me, Donna. He *paced* me."

"And you're angry about this?"

"No. Why? Do I seem angry?"

"It seems like you're having a hard time accepting it."

"I accept it. I do. I just . . ."

Now Frank was confused. He held a forkful of peas above his plate but did not bring it to his lips. It hovered there as he stared into the void, his thought unfinished.

"The weather down the shore's supposed to be gorgeous this weekend," said Donna, breaking his trance. "We couldn't have picked a better time to go."

She was very excited about seeing Francis. She had gone to the store that morning and bought him rash guards and swimmies and a pair of aqua socks. Paul had urged her not to, but she said she couldn't resist. The stuff was too cute and it was on sale. She went into the living room and came back with a large plastic bag. She showed everything to Frank, even the receipt. He commented here and there, but mainly he watched Donna: she took out each item and then placed it neatly back in the bag as if she were handling a flag or a gown. Her face beamed in the presence of these simple treasures, and Frank saw how much she loved Francis, how much she enjoyed spoiling him. Again he was struck by her beauty and her goodness, and he thanked fortune for bringing her into his life.

The plan, she said, was for Frank to come home in the morning after stopping at Janet Malloy's house. If they left before noon, they had a better chance of beating the Friday shore traffic, and maybe even getting in a few hours at the beach. Frank said that would be perfect and patted Donna's thigh.

After they ate, Frank lay on the living room floor while Donna applied the hot and cold compresses. She only did a few, as she still had some packing to get to, but they seemed more effective this time, meeting the pain whereas the day before they had barely touched it. When Frank walked out to the deck to fill the bird feeder, he noticed that he wasn't favoring his left leg as much, he wasn't limping.

He sat at the glass table and spied a squirrel creeping along the deck railing toward the feeder. Before it started nosing into the seed, Frank rapped on the glass and the sound frightened the squirrel back into the tree. He didn't mind the squirrels; he just always thought that the birds should have first crack at the feeder. He could hear them chatting not far off, but he couldn't see them. Dusk was coming on, and soon the bats would be out, black and singular against the dimming sky. The cicadas had ceased their whine and churn, and in its place rose the crickets' dominion of scratching.

On summer evenings like this one Frank would sometimes bring Paul to the old shop in Folcroft. Paul was in elementary school then, and he hadn't yet formed an opinion of his father or what he did for a living. He still wanted to be around him and go with him wherever he went. There were always rugs piled up against the back wall of the dry room in a high, sloping wedge, and Frank would let Paul climb to the top and roll down as many as time as he wanted. When Paul tired of this, he would find a nook amid the rolls and lay there catching his breath while Frank readied the moped for them. They would buzz through the neighborhood surrounding the shop, Paul in front, Frank in back, encasing the boy, protecting him. This was not the neighborhood where Paul lived, so he thrilled at seeing all the different houses and the different groups of children playing on the corner. One time they rode through a park and trundled over a foot bridge that spanned an offshoot of Darby Creek, and another time they stopped at a Dairy Queen and sat together on a parking block eating soft serve. It was like a little vacation just for the two of them.

Frank remembered quite clearly how he had felt on those evenings with his son, before the world had come between them. He loved Paul and Paul loved him. This did not need to be said or shown: it was firmer than truth— it was fact. And more, they respected each other, they each had a picture in their minds of what the other looked like, and that picture was too bright and too bold to ever be sullied. A father takes an interest in the shape of his son's heart, and the boy returns the favor, gives it back to the man, unconsciously, in so many small ways. Frank still loved his son, and he believed that Paul still loved him, but he had not given it back in many years, not in the way Frank thought he should, with honor and humility. He professed to be smarter than his father: he knew about how people are supposed to live, the right food to eat and the right products to buy, and that was the picture Paul carried around in his head, not the picture of Frank Renzetti, but of a new man, a man more like himself, at the heels of whom older men foundered, casualties of time, prostrate ideals.

CHAPTER THIRTEEN

Mr. Charleston was waiting for Frank when he pulled up to the shop early Friday morning. He jumped out of the Grumman Olson with the white towel covering his head like a bonnet. It was just past seven o'clock and he was already sweating.

"You line someone up for that rug yet?" he asked.

Frank told him about Janet Malloy and Mr. Charleston's eyes grew wide. "That's why I brought it to you," he said, slapping Frank on the back. "You know where the big fish swim."

Frank threw open the overhead door and they walked into the shaded vault of the warehouse. They went to the back of the van and Frank unrolled the Kirman to show Mr. Charleston. The junker was astonished.

"You're a magician, Frank! A god damn *magician*! Don't even look like the same rug."

"How much were you gonna charge for it at the flea market?" Frank asked as he rolled the carpet back up.

"Shit. Hundred, hundred-fifty tops."

"What do you say we charge five?"

Mr. Charleston lifted his palms in deference. "I got absolutely no problem with that number."

Frank put the Kirman back on the van. He glanced at Connie's sanctuary rug and part of him sank. Then, just as quickly, the same part leavened. The rug was the last thing standing between him and the end. As much as he disliked what it stood for, and the person for whom it was meant, it was his ticket out. Cash it in and he was off to the shore. Drip castles with Francis. Donna in her new bathing suit. The sun, the sea, the sand. *Freedom on the other side. Cool, cool release.*

He opened his wallet and counted out $50, the same money Edgar had turned down the night before. "The woman hasn't agreed to buy it yet, but I'm pretty sure she will. We've known each other a long time. Here's a little advance."

Pocketing the cash, Mr. Charleston looked around the shop with his scavenger's eye and noticed for the first time the boxy, brown mass on the floor behind them. "What do you got there?" he asked, the flea starting to itch.

"Highboy," said Frank. "Belonged to a customer's ex-husband. You can take it if you want. Have to fix it, though. I busted the leg."

"Sounds like you did it on purpose."

"I did. And I'd do it again."

With his rusty hand truck, Mr. Charleston wheeled the highboy to the rear of his van and stood it up in the street, leaning against the hobbled corner to keep it from tipping. He was very careful with the piece, very gentle. He got it inside the van by easing it onto its back and gradually sliding it across the floor, where it lay like a valley between the sweeps of junk on either side of the hold.

Frank came out with the cabriole leg and handed it to Charleston. "I'll have the rest of the money for you on Monday. I might be a little late getting in, though. Beach this weekend."

Mr. Charleston sopped the sweat from the back of his neck and jumped behind the wheel of the Grumman Olson. "When you're swimming," he said, "make sure you think of me riding around in this hot box, 'cause I sure as hell am gonna be thinking about you splashing around in that water." He honked his horn and shunted off down the street, waving the cabriole leg out the window like a prize he had just won.

THE DRIVEWAY at Connie's house was empty, and there were no trucks or vans on the street. Frank smiled: this was just how he had wanted it. Direct access to the front door and a straight shot all the way through to the sanctuary. No one to get in his way and no one to bother him. A rug man's dream.

He knocked on the door and seconds later Gildea answered in her baggy tan scrubs and white canvas bobos. Connie was out with the dog, she informed him, and the girls were upstairs getting ready. Their father would be coming soon to pick them up for the weekend. She led Frank to the sanctuary and turned on the light.

"Do you want me to sweep the floor for you?" she asked. "It's dusty."

Just four days ago, Frank would've said yes, hit the whole floor with a Swiffer, but too much had happened since then for him to care about something as trivial as a layer of dust. "It's okay," he said, then, "Elaine mentioned a pad."

"Oh," said Gildea, and from the top shelf of the closet she pulled out an off-white cocoa mat that had been sloppily folded in quarters. She gave it to Frank and they stood in silence for a moment, both of them looking at the satin-cushioned walls of the sanctum-asylum.

"I'm surprised that Connie's not here to see the rug go down," said Frank. "As much as she and Elaine fussed about it."

"She's at P.J.'s second agility test," said Gildea. "The place is over an hour away. Believe me, she wanted to be here."

Frank unfolded the mat, inhaling its strong scent of cocoa. "Thank you for saving the bedroom rug the other day."

Gildea laughed, a pleasant bounce in the back of her throat. "I almost didn't. Notice how I waited until the last minute?"

"You were going to let him do it?"

"Not because I wanted anything to happen to the carpet, and not because I wanted to make extra work for you." A devious sparkle lit up her eyes. "I did it for me."

Frank smiled appreciatively. "Your way of saying 'F you' to the boss, huh?"

"Well," she said, her small, pointy head bobbing right then left, "almost. It was more to scare her, really, but then I felt bad when she hit him and carried on like she did afterward. Though I expected that."

Frank started unrolling the perforated mat and Gildea, out of automatic courtesy, shut the closet door when she saw it was going to obstruct him. "Connie was rather sweet before the divorce," she said, edging around him noiselessly, "before the renovation. You wouldn't believe it, but it's true. Now she wants everything to be beautiful, everything perfect. It's made *her* ugly, honestly, but I could never tell her that, no matter how many times I've wanted to."

"If I told half my customers what I *really* thought of them," said Frank, but he trailed off and the two of them again were silent.

Gildea excused herself to take care of something in the kitchen. "Just yell if you need me," she said, and slipped out the double doors.

Using the tape measure he'd brought with him, Frank centered the pad in the room, shaking it left and smidging it right until its edges were exactly seven and a half inches from the surrounding baseboard. Elaine wanted six inches of hardwood showing on all four sides; in order for an area rug to stay in place, to prevent it from "walking," its underlayment should be shy of the rug's border by one and a half inches. This was also to keep the anchor from "peeking," showing its face where it wasn't wanted. Frank hated a peeker. It was one of his pet peeves, a fractional flaw that he could not suffer. Satisfied with how the non-skid pad was laying, he set the tape measure on the windowsill and went out to get the yenta's magic carpet.

The distance from the van to the front entrance was about ten yards, just far enough for Frank to start feeling the weight of the rug on his shoulder and lower back. Once he was through the open door, he kicked it closed with his heel, and in doing so lost his balance and pitched forward. The backing shredded the skin of his neck and forearm as he tried to keep the rug from shifting too much. He feared he was going to lose it, and he knew that he wouldn't be able to pick it up again if he had to lift it from the ground. The roll led him stumbling into the foyer, and he quickly looked around for something to hold onto, something to stabilize him. His eyes went to the glass finial, hesitated, zoomed in. That topaz sphere called to him like a beacon. Cold it had been all the days prior, cold and hard and dead to the touch, but now it pulsed and glowed as if lit from within, a warm, green light such as one sees in the middle of a thick fog. If only he could reach it, if only he could grip it with his free hand and lean on it for support, he might be able to make it.

His hand found the finial, and there was no resistance, no rejection: the two came together like a ball and socket. Frank held fast to it, and in the quiet following the panic he heard a car door slam and someone coming up the path in hard-bottomed dress shoes. The door opened and a man's voice said, "Let me help you with that."

Frank couldn't turn around to see who it was. He merely said, "It's okay. I got it," and adjusted the rug on his shoulder, a little hop of the roll to more evenly distribute the weight, something he had done one time if he had done it a thousand. But when he let go of the finial, the full heft of the rug again bore down on him. He felt the pressure building in the base of his spine, building, building, building, and then it was as if a shell exploded, sending shrapnel screaming in every direction. Pain, like a javelin, shot down his right leg and ground into his heel. He went blind from it, a sustained lightning flash, and he could no longer stand. Fainting, he reached for the finial, careened to the left, lost all control of the rug. The front end flew up like a see-saw, and the whole thing rode on his back, parallel with him as he crashed into the steps, his face buried in the sisal runner, his arms outspread.

CHAPTER FOURTEEN

Frank lay in a hospital bed, waiting for his day nurse to return with his cane. Having just measured him for it, she was down at the pharmacy getting it sized and cut. She wanted him to take a walk before Donna came to pick him up and bring him home. He had tried walking by himself yesterday afternoon but didn't get very far, just back and forth in the hallway outside his room. He had used a generic metal cane that was too short for him; he hoped that with a customized wooden one he'd be able to at least travel once around the fifth floor. The briskly supportive Makayla said that she wasn't comfortable letting Frank leave until he could walk, as she put it, "with confidence and purpose." Both of those things were in short supply at the moment. Frank promised her he'd do his best, whatever that was.

He took a drink of ice water and set the cup on the tray beside his bed. He looked around the room: the walls were marred with black streaks where a cart had scraped against them, and the windowpanes were dusty and spot-

ted; the recycled air was sappy, warmish, and cloyed with
the odor of dirty linen, of copper and bile. Sitting upright
in the bed, he could see the windows of another wing of
the hospital across the way, and in the foreground the
topmost branches of a courtyard tree, artificial or real he
could not say. Frank would not miss anything about this
place. It was more conducive to sickness than to health.
His packed bag had been sitting on the vinyl armchair
beneath the mounted television since early that morning.
He wished Makayla would come back soon with his cane
and his paperwork so that he could take his walk and get
the hell out of there. The longer he stayed, the worse he
was bound to feel.

FRANK HAD COME to the hospital the previous day to
have a laminotomy performed by Dr. Robert Leventhal,
an orthopedic surgeon. The Monday after his collapse,
Frank had gone to see the spry, baby-faced doctor at his
offices in Broomall, and the X-rays and MRIs and diagnos-
tics revealed that Frank had suffered a "massive" herni-
ated disk in the L5/S1 region of his lower spine. Leventhal
told him that the disk had likely ruptured months before,
which would account for his dumb and dolorous leg. It
turns out that Temoyan the chiropractor was wrong and
Gord the binder mechanic was right. Frank had had sciatica, not a pulled hamstring, as he was thumped to believe.

The slipped disk was crowding the sciatic nerve ("the
Pennsylvania Turnpike of the central nervous system," as
Leventhal explained), bumping up against it, squeezing it
on bad days. With 25 percent of the disk already extruded,
the incident at Connie's—the failure of the disk's collagen,
the nucleus pulposis, to absorb the shock of all that imita-

tion wool—caused another 25 percent to push through the
outer layer of cartilage, the annulus fibrosus. The crowd
became a rabble, the nerve pinned, choked, and thus in-
flamed. Leventhal didn't think that cortisone would be
enough to free it; they would have to open him up. Frank
dismissed the idea out of hand: he had never gone under
the knife before in his life, and wasn't about to now, with
a business to run and jobs still on the docket. But after
a long talk with Donna (at its climax, she held his face
between her hands and spoke to him softly yet sternly),
Frank capitulated, yielding to her better sense.

He went in for surgery the following week, on a Friday morning. The procedure (the sawing away of the lam-
ina, the excising of the bulging disk matter, the sealing of
the incision with glue) lasted three hours, and as he lay
in post-op next to a man who had torn his ACL in a tight-
rope-walking accident, Frank could feel—knew undoubt-
edly—that the pain in his leg was gone and would not
return. He stared up at the ceiling, a mural of sky and
cloud, and teared up, shedding more than one and caring
not who saw him.

Donna was waiting for Frank when they wheeled him
into his room, still woozy from the anesthesia. She sat
with him while he ate his lunch—arid chicken breast,
droopy asparagus, a once-burnt twice-baked potato. The
highlight was a vanilla ice cream cup, that convalescent
stand-by. The intubation tube had nicked his uvula, making it hard for him to swallow. The ice cream, cold and
smooth and sweet, went down much easier than the rest
of the meal, which he could only bring himself to pick at.

The worst part about those first few hours after surgery
was not being able to pee. The first time he tried, he knelt

on the bed with a plastic pitcher held before him like an ad hoc urinal. His urethra was still sore from the catheter, and what little fluid he did void burned as it dripped out. Makayla said that the sphincter is the last muscle to wake up from anesthesia, and this delays the body's natural ability to eliminate water. Standing at the foot of his bed and tapping the metal rail with a pen, she warned that if he couldn't successfully pee on his own, they would have to re-insert the catheter.

This was all Frank needed to hear.

He guzzled two cups of ice water and circled the room with Donna at his side, her one hand on his wrist and the other at his elbow. Makayla insisted that any amount of walking would loosen the sphincter, and she was right. He went back to the bed and triumphed, emptying 200 milliliters into the yawning pitcher. Despite Donna's objections, Frank left it on the tray for Makayla to see. She was so impressed by the volume that she didn't want to dump it out right away. To her and Frank it was a trophy; to Donna it was bedpan. Convinced that the other two would never stop marveling at it, she poured Frank's victory into the toilet and sat down herself to go to the bathroom. Something about her husband's pee in plain sight she just couldn't abide.

The ordeal left Frank tired, and he slept for an hour, though it was a fitful sleep. He woke to the IV machine announcing its dole with a beep and a gasp, and saw someone sitting next to the bed, someone he had not expected. Paul Renzetti, his face still browned from the Ventnor sun, was poised in a chair scrolling through his phone. He wore flip-flops, salmon-colored shorts, and a pressed white polo. His wavy brown hair was severely parted, but there didn't seem to be as much product in it, giving it a softness, an honesty.

"Hey," said Frank groggily.

"Hey," said Paul, pocketing his phone. "How do you feel?"

Frank rose on his elbows and Donna came around to fluff as best she could his flat plastic pillows.

"I'm okay. My back's sore from the incision, but otherwise I'm good."

Paul nodded and Frank waited for him to say something, but he was quiet.

Frank asked, "How come you didn't bring Danielle and Francis? Kids are allowed to visit."

The anti-embolism wraps on Frank's calves inflated, and the sound they made, like the filling of a balloon, drew a scientific look from Paul.

"I wasn't even going to come myself," he said. "Mom called, and I had some time, so . . ."

Frank gave his son a quick, false smile, and Paul returned it.

"Didn't he get tan?" said Donna, resting her hands on Paul's shoulders.

"It could've been you guys," he said. "We missed you down there." He strained not to look at his father.

"We wanted to go," said Donna. "Both of us, more than anything. But your father couldn't walk. He could barely move."

"And whose fault is that?"

"Nobody's. He was trying to get done early so we could come see you. He had no control over what happened."

"Of course he did. Of course he had control." Paul swung around in his seat, pinning eyes on Donna.

"Who works the way he does on one good leg? Who works the way he does on *two* good legs? Tell me that. *Tell* me!"

"Don't yell at your mother," said Frank, surprised at the strength in his voice. "You want to yell? Yell at me."

Paul faced forward again, uncowed. "I'll yell at you," he said, "but it won't do any good. You're still going to ignore everything I say and run your body into the ground. As many times as I've told you to find something else, do less, take the business in a different direction, you've never listened to me—ever! And now look at you, look what your stubbornness has done. Even Uncle John never found himself in a hospital bed. You told me yourself. Even he had the presence of mind to get out before the job broke him entirely."

"John went home to a sick wife," said Frank.

"And now Mom's going home to a sick husband. Is that what you want for her?"

Frank looked at Donna, and thought of her standing over the kitchen sink, wringing water from his compress. "No," he said. "It's not what I want."

"Then you better listen to the doctor," said Paul.

"You told him?" Frank asked Donna, and she did not meet his eyes, only stared down at the bed's crumpled sheet. He could tell that she was fed up already, that she regretted even asking Paul to come. Frank hadn't meant to accuse her, or to make her feel that she had betrayed him, because Paul was going to find out anyway; he had probably drawn the conclusion himself, before even speaking to Donna. But now that it was in front of them, Frank wanted someone to explain to him how he was supposed to follow Leventhal's decree, how he was expected, after his back had healed and he had fully recovered, to just not work anymore, to simply stop.

"You don't have a choice," Paul said. "You keep working the way you do, it's only a matter of time before it happens again. And when it does, it's going to be a lot worse—for you and Mom."

"What do you want me to do?" asked Frank. "Sell the business?"

He had said it as a joke, but when he saw the expression on Paul's face, the seriousness in his eyes, the tightening of his mouth, Frank wanted to take it back.

"Yes," said Paul. "I think it might be time."

"I wouldn't know the first thing about how to do that," Frank said.

"*I* know." Paul leaned in to touch his father's arm. "I can help you."

"It might be good, honey," said Donna.

Frank looked at her coldly. Her shoulders were hunched, her head was bent to the side, and her cheeks and forehead glowed red. Frank didn't like the shape of her smile; there was no solidarity in it.

"I'm not paralyzed," he said to her. "I'm going to be able to walk after this."

"Yes, I know that," she said. "But the way the doctor described it—it *scared* me, Frank. You lost half the disk, and what's left is no good. You say you'll take it easy, but I know you won't. You'll go back and you'll want to do it all yourself, just like you always have. You don't trust anybody else. You don't think anybody can do as good a job as you, but that's because you never had the patience to teach them."

"They never wanted to learn," Frank muttered, and these words were not just for her.

Embarrassed, Paul took his hand away and got up to look out the window.

"Billy wanted to," said Donna.

"Billy's a low-life," Frank said definitively. "Him and his nephew. Even when they were around, I was basically alone. I have been since John left."

"What about the guy from Morty's that you couldn't get over? What was his name? Edwin?"

"Edgar."

"Yes! Edgar. What about him?"

Annoyed, Frank waved her off. "He's not even documented."

"Maybe you can bring him on as, like, an unofficial partner. Is that something he can do, Paul?"

"If that's what he wants," said Paul diplomatically. "You bring him on as an *official* partner, he might be able to achieve residency status."

"And what would I do?" asked Frank. "Watch?"

"No," said Paul, turning from the window, "but you wouldn't have to work as hard. You wouldn't have to kill yourself. There's a smarter way."

"So the way I've been doing it is stupid?"

Makayla knocked on the half-open door and politely asked to see Donna in the hall. "We just need to go over some home care instructions. Nothing you need to worry about, Frank."

When father and son were alone, Frank repeated his question: "Is my way stupid?"

Paul sat back down in the chair next to the bed. He leaned forward with his elbows resting on his knees and the tips of his fingers pressed together. He looked into his father's eyes. "When I was little," he began, "I used to wait for you to come home from work. I would sit at the window and stare at the spot where you parked your van. I would get so happy when I saw you pull up, I would run through the house and hug you before you even got to the back door. It was the best part of my day, and I always looked forward to it. You were home and you were safe and you weren't going anywhere until the morning, which felt like a million years away.

"But this one time you were late coming home, hours late. Mom and I ate dinner without you and I sat at the window in my pajamas until way after dark. The longer I sat there and waited the more scared I got that something terrible had happened to you. I got it into my head that you had been kidnapped and replaced with a robot that looked exactly like you. When you finally got home, I didn't hug you or talk to you or even go near you. I was too afraid. I just watched you from afar, trying to pick up on your robot behavior—a change in your voice, a stiffness in the way you were standing.

"After a while, I got tired of watching and came up with a test to see if you were really my dad. Robots don't smell, I told myself. If I go up to him and he smells like my dad, then I have nothing to worry about. If I go over there and he doesn't smell at all, then the science fiction I've been reading is absolutely true."

"Well," said Frank, "did I smell?"

"Yeah."

"Like what?"

"Like a musty old carpet. What do you think? And when I smelled it on you, I hugged you and started crying and telling you how much I loved you and how much I never wanted anything bad to happen to you—and I still feel the same way."

"You're not embarrassed of me?" Frank asked.

"No."

"You're not ashamed?"

"No."

"You're proud of me and the life I've chosen?"

"Yes. I didn't want it for myself, but that doesn't make it stupid. A son who turns down his father's gift is still his son. Right?"

Donna returned and shut the door behind her. Frank and Paul looked over at her and she stopped at the foot of the bed, reading first her husband's face and then her son's, relieved to find there a tentative peace.

Paul received a text message. He checked his phone and texted back in a pinball of thumbs. "That was Danielle. She and Francis say hello."

Danielle had sent a picture of Francis eating his lunch of minced hot dog, and Paul shared it with his parents. He then showed them the pictures he had taken of Francis while they were down the shore. They all looked similar, with Francis either sitting or standing by the water in his little fisherman's hat and sunglasses. Donna reacted to each one as if it were its own miracle, her wonder instantly renewed. Frank, too, could feel himself wanting to reach into the phone and take the boy's hand, guide him into the water and jump him over the waves.

Such a simple thing, he thought. Am I the one who made it so hard?

As Paul and Donna were fawning over the boy, his thoughts went to Norm Kershner in his hard-bottomed dress shoes. He had come to the house on Dunwoody Lane to pick up his daughters and found himself in the sanctuary with Gildea, spreading the Timeless Peacock, a thing he did not have to do, and, on moral principle, should not have done. And then Frank thought of Elaine George, who had driven in rush-hour traffic to Chestnut Hill to deliver Janet Malloy's Kirman, and who had sat in the den of the last surviving member of the Summer Rug Gang for over an hour, talking about what could be done to sell her manor house.

They helped you, he conceded. The Lawyer and the Decorator. Stiff-necked people finished the job, bailed you out when you were sinking. It's staring you right in the face: the whole thing isn't you. It never was. As good as you are, Ace, you can't handle the sheet by yourself. There's too much of it, and too far yet to go. So let him help you. Let him walk ahead. Let him be the man he is.

THE NURSE CAME BACK with his cane. It was mahogany with a curved handle and a Nev-a-slip ferrule of tough, black rubber. She helped him to his feet and led him around the room a few times, just as Donna had done in his catheter panic. He liked the cane, but he didn't like the way it made him look: like a fragile old man. Makayla sensed this.

"You're doing good," she said, trying to cheer him up. "You don't even need me."

He walked into the hallway on his own and she came out and stood beside him, rubbing his back. "I'm going to finish your paperwork," she said. "See if you can get to the end of the hall. I'll be satisfied with that."

Frank puttered down the hall in his socks, trying not to make any sudden movements. He feared what would happen if he lost his balance, or if he put too much pressure on his lower back. He was afraid of hurting himself again. His body, once a brazen tool, had become an object of reluctance. Walking, putting one foot in front of the other, was now a voluntary act, something he had to think about, *will* himself to do. Each time he set his right foot on the ground he steadied himself, rallying what little strength he had to stay upright, centered and moving forward. This embarrassed him, angered him, and he gripped the cane tighter. Then, scared it might cause him harm, he quickly loosened his grip.

He reached the end of the hall and turned left. An orderly in blue scrubs smiled at Frank and gave him a thumbs-up as he wheeled past with a cartful of dirty dishes. Frank saluted the swift-walking man and sought a groove for his own steps, found it, and stayed inside it. He neither sped up nor slowed down, but maintained the safe, respectable pace of the student driver. His back, the core of his physical being, was tender, raw, sensitive even to the brush of fabric. Leventhal had said that sitting would be uncomfortable for the first two months; standing and walking would be better for his back, even though they required more effort. Frank felt a twinge of pain in his lumbar, and then felt it again a few moments later. He stopped. Like a child pressing his ear to the ground, he listened to his body, guiding his consciousness into the disk, spirit entering flesh. What he heard was a gentle, persistent hum, a low, thriving energy like that emitted by a pylon. But beneath that, around it and above it, he heard a bell of warning, awful in its plainness, and of these two sounds, the life of him and the death, he knew to which one he must answer, and would have to answer for the rest of his days.

Then, with a suddenness that made his eyes water and his back seize, he hacked once, twice, a third time, raking the walls of his throat as he spat into his palm a loose wet ball of greenish-yellow mucus. When he had blinked away the tears and could stand without the alarm going off too loudly in his spine, he held the wad close to his face and saw that it swam with fiber and lint, fuzz and filaments of different colors, thicknesses, and lengths: the foreign objects that had resided in his phlegm and rheum for so long that his organism no longer recognized them as foreign, had incorporated them, altered itself to accommodate them, courted and counted on them. And here it was rejecting them. After all these years, Genesis had come to her last pulled rib, the floor naked and cold, a gap, an emptiness. The rug man accepted it, wiped his palm on the hem of his gown, and continued walking.

The Oncology Ward was on the same floor as the Orthopedic Ward. To complete his lap, which Frank was now determined to do, he would have to pass through it. He noticed that this ward was much quieter than his: people kept their voices down, TVs murmured. There weren't as many visitors, either; most of the patients were alone. As he hobbled past their open doors, Frank glanced at the truly sick. In one room, a tiny old lady sat hunched in a chair, her hospital gown askew, baring one crinkly shoulder. She had a plum-colored blain that stretched across her brow, and she kept repeating the same phrase in a high monotone, "Please help me, please help me." In another room, this one gray with shadow, he saw a man in shorts and T-shirt supine on the bed. His sunken body was formless beneath his clothes. He was so emaciated that he appeared to be emerging from the sheets rather than lying atop them, as if he were in bas-relief. Whenever a nurse came out of one of the rooms, Frank's eyes would go to the floor in front of him. He felt something strong and serious in their nature that terrified him almost as much as the patients. Thank You letters pinned to a bulletin board praised these men and women, testifying to their virtue, compassion, and grace. Frank paused to read a few of them; he could not tell the names of the living from the names of the dead.

Back in his room, Frank changed out of his gown and sat on the edge of the bed with both hands stacked on the cane. It was just past eleven o'clock; Donna would be coming soon. There was nothing to do, so he looked at the painting hanging on the wall opposite the bed: Lanny Barnard's *Colors of Cozumel*, according to the placard at the bottom of the frame. It depicted a stocky, suspendered man walking alone through a coastal village, the roofs of the houses painted green and red, their doors and windows a cornflower blue. The man was seen from behind, a dark-haired figure in the near distance bearing something in his arms, a basket or a bundle. This burden was the same color as his dark brown hair, the same color as his baggy brown pants. There was no life in the village around him, no proud men or beautiful women, no children playing beneath the palms, no scrabbling chickens. All by himself on the road of yellow sand, he walked close to the brightly colored, well-kept houses, though he did not belong to them, nor them to him. He did not live in Cozumel, but in another village, a lesser place farther from the houses. That's where he's going, thought Frank—away and home.

Donna arrived and Frank was discharged without too much delay. He said goodbye to Makayla on his way to the elevator and she hugged him and kissed him on the cheek.

At his request, Donna stopped at the CVS near their house to buy Frank a bag of Chunkys and a Coke.

"Just this one time," she said, giving him the bag.

He ate two of the candies before they even got out of the parking lot. "They're still the best," he said. "I don't know why everyone hates them."

"Because they have raisins," said Donna.

"But that's what makes them so good."

He had the cane between his legs and he was looking out the window. Donna glanced over at him a few times as though she might say something. Then she asked, "Have you thought about it?"

Frank kept looking out the window. "Not since yesterday."

"I talked to Paul last night, and he said between the business and the building, you could get $400,000. And if we want, he can help us invest it."

Frank didn't say anything. He drank his soda.

"Or you can reach out to Edgar. Whatever you think is best. Whatever you want to do."

Feeling a pinch in his back, Frank wiggled this way and that to relieve it, and the cane slipped away from him. It bumped into the glove compartment and slid against the door, where he left it.

"We'll see," he said, and lightly squeezed her thigh.

She laughed at his touch, strangely, then, in a breath, lay her hand on his, palm forming to knuckles, and held him there.

photo by Debra Burke

David Amadio teaches Creative Writing and Composition at Lincoln University, America's first degree-granting HBCU. His work has appeared in *Cleaver, Packingtown Review, Adaptation, Talking River, Nerve Cowboy*, and the *San Francisco Examiner*. He belongs to a three-man comedy troupe called the Minor Prophets, which has written, directed, and produced over thirty award-winning short films. David lives in suburban Philadelphia with his wife and two children. *Rug Man* is his first novel.